STAMPEDE

BY

TERRY MAY

ROCK HILL PUBLISHING

Published by: Rock Hill Publishing

ISBN: 978-0-9831817-1-2

For My Kids

CHAPTER 1

Harvey Kitren slouched in the saddle, ready for his long ride to end. Off to the right of the trail a cliff rose up high enough to make him tilt his head back to see the top. Grass grew tall on the spring water wandering its way downhill to the river a hundred yards ahead.

You didn't smell death here now. Time and buzzards and coyotes had cleaned the flesh away and bone men had done their work for years, hauling the broken leavings off to one market or another.

First had been buffalo, running from the Apache and Comanche through the blistered heat of a hundred summers, tongues red and swollen in their open mouths, eyes white with terror; pushed to the edge of that clifftop. Harvey imagined the sounds of those times, the screams of the animals, the whoops of the Indians, the crowding from the big herd behind. Bodies falling, crashing down here, mangled and torn by the rocks, bleating, bellowing. The flow of blood from the knives of squaws.

He pulled a tobacco sack from his shirt pocket and held it in his left hand while he unpinned his Texas Ranger badge and slipped it into the same pocket. The business ahead was a private thing, requiring no authority. He left the reins slack across the horn of his saddle. The bay pony picked up his pace a little bit, scenting water. Harvey rolled and lit a smoke with a match he scratched across his boot heel, not a man to mark up a good saddle with it the way some did. He exhaled the first drag of gray tobacco smoke, less gray than the sunless day. He liked the smell of it mixed with the river smell and the grass smell and the salty sweat rising off the horse he'd never named, believing as he did that any horse had a private name of its own and no need of another.

And then the longhorns. Two different trail herds five years apart, heading another direction entirely. Moving in a slow, dry walk west to the New Mexico territory, getting a twist of that river smell on some vagrant wind, wheeling south, lusting for water and unwilling to turn. Each disaster had left its stories behind. Of the dead and dying animals piled at the foot of the high cliff. Of broken cowboys and their broken-legged ponies. Of broken-hearted ranchers standing up there on the edge looking down crying.

The Frio River ran east to west here then cut downhill a few miles farther on, fighting its way on a shallow, rocky bed toward its mergence with the Nueces. The little town on the other side was called Stampede.

CHAPTER 2

He stood on the bank and let the pony walk into the clear water alone, drinking, pausing and drinking again, bridle reins loose and afloat. Harvey flipped the last of his smoke into the water and watched it bounce off a cypress knee then head downriver, coming apart and losing itself in the current. He clucked his tongue and the pony came up the bank and waited, dripping water off his mouth and legs. Harvey caught the wet reins and remounted.

This made his third trip down here. First time, he was one of the riders fighting to turn the lead steers away from that tall cliff. Everybody knew what you had to do in a case like that. Nose them around and run them back into each other, roll them into a wheel spinning on itself til they tired down and quit. He'd done it a dozen times but that time it had not worked. At the end of the long night, half the herd destroyed on these rocks, he and the others had watched his trail boss stand at the edge with his hat off, not making a sound, tears breaking the cake of dust on his face.

But that was long years ago. No town here then. Nearest was Encina that later got itself named Uvalde after some Mexican governor. Harvey had nothing against governors, but he thought Encina a better name.

His second trip here had turned out futile and left him with a heavy heart and a private anger that had never burned itself out. That had been, how long now? Three years? Yes, it was three years.

Now this.

He rode to the cemetery first. Set on high ground above river floods, it had been here longer than the town, begun after the first bad stampede left two men dead. Then later, his bunch.

Only one man from Harvey's crew had died that night, but it had been a hurtful loss. Just a kid, a laugher and a poker of fun that everybody liked. What was the boy's name? Andy. Andrew something. There was a cross at the head of the boy's grave now, whitewashed like the others.

A cedar-picket fence enclosed the place, with a gate on iron hinges and a peaceful feel to it in the shade of big oaks that probably had tap roots clear down into the river bed. Just one new grave, freshly dug and off to itself in the back beside another one that had been there a longer while. Unlike the other graves, those two were not graced by crosses or any other sort of marker. He'd have to see to that while he was here. There'd been a rain or two on it since it was filled in. The mounded dirt had begun to sink and grass was reaching into it. Harvey took off his hat and stood at the foot of it, remembering back to the years he and the woman who was buried here had played together; barefoot, young and ignorant of the world; but like young Andy over in the corner there, laughers and pokers of fun. He made not a sound, but like his old trail boss, and no doubt other men and women since, he felt hot tears mark their way through the dust on his face and drop to the waiting ground.

CHAPTER 3

The town was one dusty street lined by a few board constructions with painted signs and hitch rails. It was a low town, everything single-story except the saloon down at the end. The *Frio*, according to its sign. Named after the river it stood beside. It was three stories high. He smelled cooking in the air and realized he was hungry. Nothing to eat since breakfast, and that had been a hurried cup of coffee and two cold biscuits when he broke camp at daybreak. Another of the signs marked a cafe halfway down the street. Looked like a crowd was headed for it. He decided to wait.

A street intersected this one and led back a few hundred yards to a cluster of shacks. Well, to be fair, they were not all shacks. A few were better than that, with fences around them. A church stood off by itself with a cross on top like the ones in the cemetery. A mixed flock of sheep and goats grazed in the curve of the river where grass grew best.

He tied his horse to a rail outside one of the picket fences. The fence looked freshly whitewashed. The house was unpainted, baked gray in the South Texas sun. No other horses tied there now, but it was early in the day. All around the rail the alkaline dirt was compacted hard as rock. Not a blade of grass or a weed grew in it. He thought it looked much like he felt.

A colored woman answered his knock. She wore a starched blue dress with a white apron over it and a white shapeless hat on her head. She offered him the same smile all men got at this door and stepped back. "Good day, sir. Come in."

He smelled coffee and frying meat. The room was empty. The woman waited for his request.

"I need to see Miss Lou."

9

Her brow wrinkled and she shook her head ever so slightly. "Miss Lou ain't up and about yet."

"It's the middle of the day."

She grinned, then put it away. "Don't matter. You know Miss Lou you know she git up and about when she please."

He kept hold of her eyes. "You go get her and tell her Harvey Kitren is out here waiting on her.

"That you, sir?"

"That's me."

She worked it through her head for a few silent seconds, running the name past memories until it snagged on one. "See what I can do."

CHAPTER 4

The woman came through the door carrying a cup of coffee in her hand, looking back and saying, "In a damned minute, Clara. I can't do but one thing at a time." She turned her bony face to Harvey. Tall, all her body like her face—angles and bone under uncombed red hair. Her skin was as white as the fence, most of it covered by pink silk. She sat down beside him like she was tired, a little groan of effort. "I figured we'd be seeing you right about now," she said.

He smelled last night's perfume. The words of the letter she'd sent passed through his thoughts. Words as sharp as barbed wire. She drank some of the coffee and put down the cup on a tiny round table beside the chair. She smiled at him with yellow teeth that caused him to wonder if she'd ever been pretty.

She said, "You talk to the sheriff?"

"Yes." He'd stayed up in Uvalde for a useless half day of questions.

"So you know already they ain't got no idea who it was done it."

He nodded his head and moved his Stetson from one knee to the other, then used the index finger of his right hand to smooth down his dark mustache.

"Yes, ma'am, I know the bare details of it, but I want you to show me where they found her. Anything else you can tell me."

She picked at a gold chain that hung around her neck. "Up in her room. Prissy found her. They was best friends. I expect she'd be the one to talk to."

"Can I come up there and see it?"

She got her coffee in hand and stood up. "Follow me."

11

A carpet runner muffled their footsteps climbing the stairs. He heard a couple of female voices in conversation behind a closed door and picked up the scents of sweat and soap in the hallway. He remembered his last visit here, the shouts and ugly words from his own mouth and from behind his sister's painted lips. And finally the rough hands of Fisher Greene around his neck, the peacekeeper doing his job. It was right about here that Harvey had planted an elbow in the big man's belly then followed his tumble down the stairs and pistol-whipped him til the women shamed him to a stop and sent him away.

Lou Campbell opened one of the doors. "In here."

"Greene still work for you?"

"He never did work for me. We was partners in it. But no, I bought him out a while back."

"Still in town?"

"Yeah. You worried about him?" She smiled her stained smile.

Harvey ignored the question. He looked around the room. Not very big, just enough space for the double bed, a narrow dresser with a tall, cloudy mirror, and a wardrobe against the far wall beside the open window. White curtains lifted and fell back in a shifting breeze.

A chamber pot hid under the edge of the bed, in a glaze of white and blue, almost covered by the oversized quilt. Two embroidered pillows waited against the headboard. A cane-seated chair backed up to the foot. Beside the dresser a spindly table held a tin wash basin and water pitcher. A white towel hung on the wall behind it.

He nodded toward the wardrobe. "Clothes still in it?"

"Nothing's been touched in here. I left it for you."

"I'll need a day or two to look through it."

"Sure. Take your time. Be another week or more before I need the room."

"What about that woman? Prissy, you said."

"Yeah. Does it have to be today? We'll get some customers in here pretty soon now."

"I won't take long."

"All right, then. I'll get her."

He slid the wardrobe open and looked at the clothes hanging inside. Long dresses with ruffled lace down the front, gingham prints and plain skirts and blouses. House coats and flimsy wearings that caused a fresh surge of anger. The things his sister had worn during these years of his absence. All of the days since he'd knocked Fisher Green down the stairs and pistol-whipped him and ridden away in a fury that would not dim. A shame that would not lift. During all the days of knowing that his sister was a whore by choice, selling herself to any whisky-soaked fool with a dollar in his hand. He stared at the edge of the bed and pictured her as she sat there wiping tears off her face, back those three years ago, not meeting his eyes. *Thank God,* he'd said. *Thank God our mama and daddy ain't here to see what's become of you.*

And his words had made no difference. Changed nothing at all. She had refused to come with him and he had refused to look back. Now this.

CHAPTER 5

A new rug softened the plank floor in front of the dresser, its colors still bright. He opened the top drawer. The smell of toilet water and powder rose out of it, small bottles shifted. One fell over and rolled against the side of the drawer. He set it upright. Some kind of pills for female complaints.

"She was on that rug where you're standing." He hadn't heard the door open. "Well, not that one. That one is new. They throwed away the old one, bloody like it was." Harvey thought the woman resembled Ella, the way she stood off at a kind of an angle, looking at him across her shoulder. She had on a shiny red housecoat and slippers.

"You Prissy?" He didn't remember seeing her last time.

"Priscilla. Customers treat me better if it's Priscilla. Name like Prissy, sounds like they can get away with things."

"I heard you was the one found Ella."

A hand came up to her breast. Her eyes searched the floor like she'd lost something there. The vision he'd handed her was stark and ugly. She nodded and went over to the chair. The hand stayed at her breast when she sat.

"We had a trail bunch in the house." Her lips clamped down as they will when fighting off a hateful memory. She looked up then and her eyes turned sharp. "They was stacked three-deep downstairs. Ella disappeared. I come looking for her."

Harvey kept quiet and let her move along at whatever pace she wanted. "There she was," pointing at his feet. "Cut up bad and bled to death." He waited on her, but she'd come to the end of it.

"Miss Lou said you two were friends."

She nodded, like her mind was elsewhere. The hand moved to her hair and began wrapping a long strand of it around a finger.

"You got no idea who it was did it?"

"Nope. I mean she was up here with Luther Welty a little while before. Luther was a regular of hers. A deputy went out and talked to him, I heard. But Luther wouldn't of done something like that. He's just another ignorant, good-hearted cowhand." Her eyes focused on him.

"You got makin's in that pocket? I could use a smoke."

He took out the sack and the book of papers and handed them to her. She was quick with it and had one rolled and hanging in the corner of her mouth in a few seconds. He lit it for her with one of his matches. He blew out the match and looked for a place to put it, didn't see anything, stuck it along with the Bull Durham sack in his shirt pocket. The smell of burned sulphur bloomed for a couple of seconds and drifted away. The Sheriff in Uvalde had mentioned Welty. Nobody thought he was the killer, but Harvey planned to make up his own mind about that.

"You were her friend, you say. Lou said it, anyway. How come she wouldn't give it up? This life here." He felt ashamed of the question, and hadn't meant to speak it, but it was a question that had chewed at him all these years and it kind of leaked out, without him knowing how. She didn't answer it for a long time. He held his breath and waited. The woman drew on her smoke again, and when she talked, the smoke shaped her words, like the dots and dashes of the telegraph code.

"She loved you more than anything. But I guess you know that, don't you?"

Oh, me was his thought. He turned away, and stayed watching out the window til the mist cleared off his vision. He nodded. "I thought so once. A long time ago. Seemed like it changed somewhere along the line. Right now, I couldn't tell you what I think."

"It never changed. I would say that life may have covered it over with calluses, like the hand of a working man, but it never

15

changed. She always talked about you. She was always proud of you."

"And she stayed a whore." He hated what he'd said, and for a second or two he hated himself for saying it. Then he hated the other woman, the whore sitting in the chair and talking to him like real women talked. Decent women who lived a long way off from fancy houses and hell-raising cowboys.

CHAPTER 6

Lou Campbell stepped through the door and said, "Need you downstairs, Prissy. There's customers just rode up." Harvey looked through the window again and saw two men tying horses beside his. Behind him the room went empty except for the trace of tobacco smoke still in the air.

He stayed put long enough for the talk and the laughs downstairs to taper off and for the sound of boots to finish their stomp down the hall outside his shut door. Other men's faces and other men's eyes inside this house carried a nearly hidden shame that he didn't want to see. There'd been a time. He'd lived through some years, back before he'd grown out of it, part of the cow crowd, part of the whisky and whores and guns, and he knew all about the secret shame men carry. Now he was a different man, changed by the circumstances of life. The same urges lived in him as always, the pull of it sometimes hard to resist, but the difference now was that he did resist it. He was on the side of the law, and not just the laws that men laid out. No, there were God's laws, too, and there was right and wrong.

You lived your life and you stayed with right. And just because you had a dollar in your pocket gave you no license to take your fun on a man's sister. On a mother's child.

Lou Campbell waited for him at the foot of the stairs. She had a fresh cup of coffee in her hand and a mocking smile on her face. Down here the smell of coffee tangled with perfume and sweat. And this is how Ella had lived. With these smells and these grins. Trading everything she'd ever had or been for dollar bills and silver coins. He wanted to burn it down.

"Who would I talk to about the grave?"

"The undertaker's up in Uvalde. Comes down in his buggy when we need him. Why?"

He ignored the question. "Who runs the cemetery? Takes care of it?"

"Why, it's that pack of Holy Rollers over yonder." She gave up the smile.

"The church I passed?" He walked to the front door and opened it. The white building was maybe a quarter mile away. "I don't remember seeing it last time I was here."

"No." She walked over to him and opened the door wider, like she was encouraging him to go on and leave. "Parson used to hold his meetings at the laundry across from the saloon on Sundays, preached on the street a while, got him a flock together and built that thing. They do the buryin', pull weeds and whitewash the fence, all that business. We got the whole shebang here now. Man can do his sinnin' with me and my girls, then run over there to pray about it. Fisher used to say he'd like to put in a toll road between us."

She finished her coffee and smacked her lips. "Amos Brace. That's the preacher. What you want with him?"

"All the graves but Ella and somebody beside her got crosses on 'em. I want to get that straightened out."

The woman's laugh came quick, and it was genuine, not something made up to cover nerves or fear. She nearly dropped her coffee and began to cough.

He could still hear her laughing behind the shut door when he left.

CHAPTER 7

Nobody was inside the church building. His bootsteps echoed off the walls. The scent of old paper drifted around him from hymnals on the benches where the listeners sat. He noticed two bibles that somebody probably forgot and left behind, bound in black leather with gold words stamped across their covers.. He picked up a book from the top of a stack beside one of the benches and thumbed it open. The pages were creased and torn. A book of songs, some he could recall from his young years. Up front was a wooden platform meant to hold a speaker off the floor above the heads of the congregation. He set the hymnal down and walked out the door. Behind the building he found nothing but an outhouse and three sheep that had grazed their way back there. The sheep noticed him, ran off a few paces and went back to cropping grass. Harvey remembered that he was hungry and headed for the cafe he'd noticed riding in.

The street was sandy, lined with wagon tracks and pocked with the prints of horse hooves and boots. He wondered again, as he had those few years ago, how the sand came to be here in the middle of limestone and cactus. Had to've been the river brought it, he supposed. In times of flood. He put off his own meal long enough to locate a stable at the far end of town.

"I'll leave him with you the rest of today and tonight, anyhow," he told the white-haired man who came out to meet him. "Give him some corn if you've got it. Can you keep the long gun for me?"

"It'll be here when you want it. Got plenty of corn. Oats, too. I'll take good care of him. How about his shoes?"

This fellow looked to be sixty years old or more, but his arms and shoulders were heavy with muscle. His short beard

19

was as white as his hair. The hand that took hold of the reins was thick and powerful. He wore the short leather chaps that horseshoers used to protect their legs. A wooden sign nailed beside the front door said *blacksmith and stable*. Black letters on a tired gray board. Harvey smelled the smoke from a forge.

"You shoe many?" Harvey didn't like just anybody fooling with his pony's feet. He'd seen many a good mount lamed by impatient work.

"I surely do. You can ask around." The man's grin exposed white teeth that looked strong enough to crack a walnut. He put out a hand. "Caudel's the name. Ed Caudel."

The grip of it felt as rough and hard as seasoned firewood. It was a hand that had done hard work. And it felt like a hand you could trust. "Kitren. They're wore down some. New ones wouldn't hurt. Why don't you go ahead and do it." He took the saddlebags and slung them over his shoulder. Inside the bags were some clean clothes, a straight razor, a wad of cash money from his last pay, a tin can for boiling coffee and an old cavalry mess kit from the war. The leather smelled like horse sweat. He turned to leave and felt his boot heels sink into the aggravating sand. The blacksmith was leading his pony to a gate that opened into a corral where a dozen animals wandered.

"Meant to ask you," Harvey said. "You know where I can find a place to stay the night?"

"Most folks put up at the saloon. They got rooms upstairs."

"Yeah, well, let's say if it was you and you needed some sleep."

There was that grin again. "I know what you mean. Woman named Morgan keeps a sort of boarding house down yonder across from the church. You might could get a bed there."

CHAPTER 8

When he reached the boardwalk that fronted the main part of this little town the walking was easier. The house Caudel mentioned had to be close to Lou Campbell's place of business. Walking felt good. He'd been riding many an hour, and though it was something he liked and was used to, it was a pleasure to stretch his legs.

The cafe's screen door banged shut behind him and the cowbell hanging on it caused the few people inside to glance at him. He took off his hat and went to an empty table in the far corner. It looked about the size to fit one or two people. He could smell the yellow oilcloth that covered it. The saddlebags went under it at his feet.

A heavy man of middle age set a steaming cup in front of him. Coffee. "Figured you'd want that." His face was friendly and tired. A crowd of people had come through here for the last hour or two. He wore a dirty white apron down to his knees.

"You read me right, mister. What's good? I could eat about anything, I'm so hungry."

"I believe there's a stewed possum left back there."

"Except that."

"And a horse flank."

"I've eat horse before. Bring it out."

"Would you settle for a beefsteak? I've got plenty."

"Now you mention it, that sounds good. Can you fry up some potatoes with it?"

He nodded and said, "Couple of eggs?"

"Sold. I'll take the whole pile. Two or three biscuits wouldn't hurt my feelings." He hung his hat on the wallpeg behind him, sipped his coffee and waited. Not many customers now. Most of the other tables were empty. A young woman wiped the counter with a wet rag and dragged stools back into order. She wore a plain dress covered by another stained apron. Her hair was coal black in a single braid down her back. Pretty girl. Conversations rose and fell in the background.

He spent a half hour at the meal. It was the first good feed he'd had in three days. He'd almost finished it when the heavy man came through from the kitchen without his apron on. The room was empty except for Harvey and two others. "I'm gonna go see about her," he said to the young woman. She waved to him as he left and walked over to Harvey's table.

"Can I get you anything else?" She had one of those low voices you heard now and then. Pretty, like her face and figure.

"Believe I'd like a slice of pie, you got any hid out."

"How about some blackberry cobbler?"

"If it's the best you can do." He smiled at her and got one back. Nice one, too. Why couldn't Ella have settled for something like this? Waiting on tables, wiping counters, serving up cobbler? Hell, anything but—the old knots showed up again in his shoulders. "Another half-cup of coffee would be good, too."

The cobbler made him think of home and the good things his mother had always fed her family. He and barefoot Ella and their father. The smell of wood smoke from the stove. And laughter.

He paid the girl and hoisted the saddlebags. "Blacksmith said there's a place rents out rooms back over yonder. Woman named Morgan. Can you point me at the house?"

"Sure. It's right behind the general store on the corner. No fence around it, and it's not painted like some of them are. A little rundown, really, but it's clean. And a sight quieter than some places I could name. I have a room there myself."

Harvey could deny it all day long, but that bit of news caused his tired old heart to skip a beat. "Much obliged."

"Morgan's her first name. Morgan Bailey. She's a widow lady."

He'd liked to've known the young woman's name, too, but thought better of asking.

CHAPTER 9

The house smelled old. He paid for a week, though not sure he'd be around that long. The bed looked clean and inviting. The big meal had him feeling heavy and drowsy. An hour or two on that mattress seemed like a good idea.

"Water well's out back of the house," she told him. It belongs to me—to this property —but I share it with some of the stores along the street. They pay me a little to draw water there, so don't start shooting if you have to get in line a time or two." She was a short woman who'd been a looker once upon a time. There was a little bit of a hump in her back, causing her to bend forward. Her hair was dark gray and kept in a bun. Shallow lines criss-crossed her cheeks. She took careful steps walking.

"Rent covers one meal a day. We eat at six in the evening. There's sometimes coffee made at sunup. More than that, you'll have to scout out on your own. The little shed behind the well is for boarders. I keep two or three tubs in it for baths if you're inclined. Shut the latch if you get naked out there. I have women stay here, too, though they might not raise much fuss, a young fellow like you." Her face lit up and she laughed. "Sissies heat their water on the kitchen stove. Outhouse is over on the other side of the lot. I change out the bed sheets once a week. If you make a mess or need a clean towel I keep a stack of fresh things out on the screen porch. That covers it, I reckon." She reminded Harvey of a clucking hen.

When she shut the door he felt the pull of the bed. He unbuckled his gunbelt and hung it over the headboard. A quilt covered a clean, white sheet and two pillows. He folded it back, let his boots hang over the side and slept crossways on it for two hours.

He knew, before his eyes opened, that he felt better. The tightness in his neck had dissolved and the headache that had been with him for two days had lifted. Only trouble was, he couldn't remember for a few seconds where he was or what he was doing there. It all came back to him quick enough, though. He raised his head and looked around the room. In the corner was a washstand that held a shallow tin bowl like the one he'd seen upstairs at Lou Campbell's. A mirror hung on a swivel at the top of the stand. He rubbed a hand over his whiskers. When had he shaved last? Or bathed, for that matter.

Morgan Bailey had a fire in the stove and a couple of pots on it. The kitchen smelled good and he was already hungry again. "Could I borrow an edge of that hot stove and a pot to heat water in?"

She brought a big teakettle out of a cabinet. "Most everybody uses this."

Harvey filled it from the water bucket and said "I'll be back in a minute. Think I'll drag in one of the tubs you talked about."

"Take that bucket with you. I'll be needing more water."

He drew a full bucket for her and took it inside, then went back to the shed for a tub and another empty bucket. It would take two or three trips before he had enough for a decent bath.

By the time he got it all ready the kettle he'd left on the stove was boiling. When he went for it the old woman grinned at him and said, "You're pretty handy to have around."

He shaved first and stayed in the tub until the water turned cold. The fit was tight. A bigger man would have been hard put to get in the thing. Harvey was not short, but he was lean as a jackrabbit and he had never had trouble with a number two tub.

Footsteps sounded up and down the hall outside his room while he got into the clean shirt and pants. He swapped pockets with the ranger star. Probably best to keep it with him. On occasion people needed to see it in order to tamp down foolish impulses, and it seemed likely there'd be some of that before he left.

His skin still felt damp from the bath and carried the smell of lye soap. He felt cleaner on the outside than inside, but once

24

he found the man who'd murdered Ella, once he rode out of this town and back into his normal life he believed time would heal the pain and the remorse, the fury and the confusion. Time was his hope and his faith.

CHAPTER 10

A man stood when he walked into the room and stretched an arm across the table. It was a long arm, like the man. Skinny and eager. "Come on in. Have a seat. I'm Dave. Dave Mikeska." The hand Harvey shook was thin, with long fingers that bore no calluses. The grip was friendly.

"Kitren. Glad to meet you." He pulled back a chair and they sat across from one another. Nobody else had come in. The table was set for five people and stacked with bowls of steaming food. Morgan Bailey brought another one in and set it down. Harvey smelled steak.

"That's fresh-killed venison," she said. "Cee brought it in this morning."

Harvey didn't know who Cee was and didn't ask. "More people coming, I hope. This's too much for two of us." He was thinking of the young woman from the cafe.

Dave Mikeska laughed and said, "In a minute. This is everybody's favorite time of day." He paused and rubbed at his chin. "You with us for a while?"

"A week maybe," Harvey said.

"Plan to settle in Stampede?"

"No sir." Cloth brushed his chair. He turned to see her go past and into the kitchen, long braid of hair still in place. Heard her talking, and the rattle of glass and cup. She set a cup of coffee at one of the empty places.

She smiled at Harvey and said, "That's for me. There's water and sweet milk to drink, too. You want a glass of milk, Dave?"

The skinny man said, "Surely do." She looked at Harvey again with a raised eyebrow.

"Same as you," he told her.

When she left the table Dave said, "She helps Morgan out with things. I guess for some of her rent." Harvey didn't comment. Two other people came into the room—a man and woman. The man sat down beside Dave Mikeska and the woman beside Harvey. That put her between him and the young lady he wanted to learn about who just then brought the coffee he'd asked for.

Their landlady joined the table at last, said a quick grace and they passed the food around. Conversation flew past him. Harvey observed silence for the most part except when asked a direct question, which he answered as near the truth as he wished to go and in as few words as possible. They were curious about him, of course, showing up the first time at the dinner table as he had. He learned that the woman next to him, who was a middle-aged Mexican, was named Rosa something, and the man across the table was Caesar Tims. That would be the *Cee* who killed the deer on which they made their supper. The man wore his hair long and had a lazy way about him.

Morgan Bailey announced Harvey to the others, said he'd be with them for a week or so, and was a handy fellow with a water bucket.

What he didn't hear, and most wanted to, was the name of the pretty woman who'd served him cobbler at the cafe and coffee right here, and who sat very quietly at her meal.

They finished with the same cobbler he'd had at the cafe earlier. Her long braid touched his shoulder as she put the bowl down. "I cooked enough for both places," she said. "Hope you don't mind."

"Oh, no. It's too good to mind." He smiled back at her and watched her sit down again. Next thing he knew, he was saying, "I'm Harvey Kitren, ma'am. Can I ask your name?" He felt his face flush and hoped nobody noticed. The woman looked up and paused, thinking something through. She swallowed, then reached for her coffee.

"Katy," she said, and sort of smiled, then covered it with the cup. Some kind of wall had gone up. He almost asked for the rest of it—her last name, too—but no. She didn't want to know him better. And she didn't want him to know her better, either. The knowledge embarrassed him more. He Left half the bowl of cobbler uneaten.

CHAPTER 11

Harvey cleaned his revolver, passing the time, wide-awake from the afternoon nap, hearing footsteps in the hall and now and then a laugh. He felt bad about the girl—Katy, she'd said—he'd been too forward and put her off, it looked like. Just as well. He'd invited no women into his life in a long time for good reason. He led a dangerous life. Now, here in Stampede, he sought answers to Ella's murder. And murder it was. This was no time to let some pretty face get in the way of that.

As he strapped on his gunbelt somebody knocked at his door. He opened it and found the young woman standing there.

"You're Ella's brother," she said. He stood back, but she didn't come inside. She'd changed into a different dress and combed out her hair. It hung past her shoulders like a dark waterfall. Harvey had never given himself to any person or any illusion before, but felt the sharp and sudden pull of this pretty young woman. He got a deep breath and willed the feelings away.

"Yes, ma'am."

"The ranger."

"You knew my sister?"

"Not very well, and not long. But yes, we talked a little."

He opened the door wider. "You want to come in? I'll leave the door open." Her eyes were pale blue.

"No, thanks. I wanted...I just wanted to tell you that I'm Katy Wallace." He thought more was coming, and something was wrong, because a tear, a single tear, came from each of those pale blue eyes and rolled down her cheeks past the corners of her mouth.

"Well, it's good to meet—"

29

She turned and walked away and after a while Harvey realized he was alone. He finished with the gunbelt, then wandered down the hall and out the front door. No moon lit the night. Lamps flickered in the windows of houses, but the stores along the street were dark. At the end of the street the saloon sparkled and sent the smell of kerosene to mingle with the smell of river water and sand and cooling trees. His boots seemed loud on the sidewalk. Why had that woman—that girl—come to his door? And why should he care, anyway?

Inside, the talk was loud and the air was heavy with burned lamp oil and beer. A sprinkle of sawdust softened footsteps. Ten or twelve men sat at tables with cards in their hands or stood belly up to the bar. All but a couple of them looked like working cowhands, dressed in range clothes. In here for a little fun after a hard day. On one of the walls hung a big painting of a near naked woman stretched out on a divan. Horns hung on the walls, too. Buffalo and longhorns and two racks of deerhorn. One of them extra big. He counted 14 points. Behind the long polished bar stood a tall man whose name he knew— Dave Mikeska.

"How about a shot of rye?" Mikeska had a smile in place and a big rag in his hand. He wiped the bar in front of Harvey. "On the house, this bein' your first time in."

"That's kind of you. But no, I'd prefer a mug of beer if you got it."

"Oh, sure. We manage to keep it cool." He brought a dark brew topped by white foam and set it down. He waited while Harvey sipped a taste. "You enjoy your supper?"

There was some sort of comment hidden in the question, like the man wanted to say more. "I did. Miz Bailey knows what she's doing." Harvey drank half the mug in one swallow. The beer stung the back of his throat. "You own this place? Work here?"

Mikeska laughed and ran the rag over a wet spot on the bar. "Just labor back here behind the bar," he said. "Been the night man for half a year now. I shut it down about midnight and head back down the street to my room. Exciting life I live. You want another beer?"

"This'll be plenty. You know a man named Fisher Greene?"

"Well, sure. Everybody knows Fisher. Hard not to know him if you live in Stampede. Runs this saloon for Mister Raines."

"He around tonight?"

"Fisher? Don't know. I ain't seen him. May be upstairs. He keeps a room on the second floor. I can go see if you want."

Harvey considered it. "Thanks, no. I'll catch him another time. You said Raines? Owns this?" Mikeska nodded. "He live here, too?" Harvey had no particular reason for asking, but this is what it would take—asking and poking around until something poked back.

"Oh, no. Raines is a rancher. Big spread lower down the Frio. I hear they found silver on it, too. The Double R they call it. This is just some place to stash his money, I guess. Don't come around much."

Something seeped into Mikeska's expression. "I could see you was taken by Katy at supper..." Harvey waited through a long silence. "But, there's things—"

"Dave!" One of the card players yelled out from a corner table. "Git over here. We need a bottle!" The chore seemed to relieve him. He glanced back at Harvey and hurried across the floor. Harvey expected the man to come back and finish whatever he'd been trying to say, but it didn't happen. Mikeska found ways to avoid more conversation until Harvey drank the last of his beer, wiped his mustache, left money on the bar and walked out. This was not the first time he'd heard the Double R mentioned. The Uvalde sheriff had gone out there to question Luther Welty. The sheriff was sure the cowboy was innocent, and it was probably a waste of time to talk to him again, but Harvey decided on a ride downriver at sunup anyway. See what Luther had to say.

High above him, as he waded through the pool of light leaking onto the sidewalk, a pair of hard eyes watched until he disappeared into the night.

Fisher Greene stepped back and let the curtains fall together. "It's him, all right," he said. "Lookin' to stir up trouble, no doubt." The woman who lay across his bed said nothing in reply.

CHAPTER 12

Harvey beat daylight onto the street come morning, the saddlebags over his shoulder again, listening to thunder stumble around the hills off to the west. Maybe not such a good morning to go riding, but a little rain wouldn't hurt him. Wouldn't hurt the dry countryside, either. Signs of drought pocked the land with dead brush and the thin crowns of dying trees out there. Now and then a blade of lightning split the dark morning, too far off to light his way. He smelled rain, and the air that carried the scent brought with it a little of the fall season just now starting to settle in.

Stables got an early start, too, with men needing their horses and horses needing their feed. The stable was well lighted, coal oil lanterns hanging on the walls. Conversation matched the intermittent growl from the distant thunder. Two men stood inside talking to Caudel, with his white beard and his white smile. He saw Harvey walk in and came to meet him.

"I didn't put the shoes on yet. Meant to do it first thing this morning."

Harvey said, "Do I smell coffee?"

"Pot's on the forge over yonder. Cafe ain't open yet, so I like to make it for my early customers. You got a cup?"

Harvey bent over and came up with the cup from his mess kit. The pot was one of those blue enameled, black-speckled ones that looked about a hundred years old, dented and scorched, sitting propped at an angle on the side of the forge. Hot coals snapped at each other inside the metal box. The coffee tasted pretty good, with a bare hint of horse sweat and hay.

He swallowed a hot dose of it and noted that the grounds hadn't all settled yet. "You needn't worry about the shoes just now. I decided to run down south, but I'll bring him back tonight or in the morning."

"Whatever you want. Let me see to these other folks and then I'll fetch your boy for you."

The men went toward the back. He sipped at the thick coffee and listened to the movements of horses, flanks rubbing on walls, shod feet clipping against feed troughs and closed gates. Snorts and deep mumbles. Another man walked in out of the dark.

The lantern light flickered. Cee, from last night's table, nodded at him and said good morning. The man wore a buckskin jacket with fringes on the sleeves and beadwork across the front of it. A coonskin cap. He put out a hand. "We had supper together last night. I'm Caesar Tims."

Harvey shook the offered hand. "Kitren. Glad to meet you."

"How do you like Ed's awful coffee?" The man had brought a tin cup with him. He poured it half-full and tasted it. He was not from around here. That accent came from somewhere north.

Harvey said, "I won't criticize free coffee."

Tims laughed. "Don't worry, he'll tack it on your bill some way. You enjoy the meal? Morgan is a damned fine cook, I think."

"I think the same as you. She said you supplied the venison."

"A little three-pointer. Walked out of the brush as I was setting up for the day. Might as well had a sign on him said *shoot me*." He drank more of his coffee. "You look like you're about to take an early ride." The accent was yankee, midwest maybe, and the attitude was nosy. Tims was an inch or two shorter than Harvey and ten years younger. His arms under the buckskin looked heavy with muscle. Harvey took a while to respond.

"That's right." He finished the coffee and dumped the grounds out of his cup.

"Which way you headed?" Tims knew how to get on a man's nerves, all right.

34

"South."
"Along the river?"
"Mostly, I guess."
"Well, me too. Mind if I ride with you?"

CHAPTER 13

His pony was full of energy from his rest and good feed. Harvey had to work at holding him back. They stayed on the south side of the Frio and kept an eye on the clouds building in the western sky. He wore the yellow slicker that he kept rolled inside his bedding and lashed behind the saddle. The rain hadn't started yet but it was about to.

"Mind if I call you by your first name, Mister Kitren?"

Well, the truth was that Harvey did mind. He didn't pass out his first name to most people, and never to nosy people like this one. He didn't like his name, and often wondered why his folks had picked it. For better or worse, though, it was his, and while Caesar Tims was an irritating man, there was no point in being rude.

"Harvey."

Tims nodded and smiled, his body moving with his horse's gait. "Everybody calls me Cee. Caesar is an unwieldy name."

They rode in silence then for many minutes. The rain came on, light at first, then heavier. Tims' buckskin jacket turned dark as water soaked into it. The fringes did their job, rain sluicing off them. Lightning hit a tree somewhere on the other side of the river and the crash of it spooked the horses. Harvey's pony calmed fast, but the heavy-footed sorrel under Tims reared so high he nearly tumbled over backward. Dangerous behavior that could do harm to a rider. The man lost his coonskin cap but clung close to the big neck, one hand in the mane, and used his weight to bring his mount down on four feet.

Harvey leaned over and lifted the cap off the cedar limb that had caught it. He rode close and handed it to Tims, who smiled despite it all.

36

"He's rented from Caudel or I'd shoot him," he said, but it was an obvious joke and he appeared to be an even-tempered man. Harvey liked him a little better, but wished he'd fork off soon to his own destination. They passed under a thick canopy of live oaks. The heavy rain fell in sheets all around, but here it only dripped, leaving a nearly dry expanse.

Harvey reined up and stepped to the ground. He dropped the reins and his pony began to crop grass. He wanted a smoke, and there was no way to roll one with it coming down like that. Tims saw him and turned back. The man had to raise his voice to be heard over the storm. "You plan to stay here?"

"Might wait for it to slack up some."

"I'd better go on. I'm worried about my stuff in this rain." He didn't explain and Harvey didn't ask. Once the sorrel was out of sight the dry spot began to seem homey. Dead leaves shifted and snapped under his feet and offered up their tannic scent. Harvey leaned against an oak and finished the smoke. The Frio was no more than twenty paces away and it looked to be up. It moved fast and was on a romp. Maybe this rain was a drought-breaker.

CHAPTER 14

The thunder and lightning switched to the east now and the rain went with it. The sky turned lighter. He mounted up and rode out into the open and headed downriver again with his slicker back in the bedroll. He gave no more thought to Tims other than to note an occasional hoofprint in the muddy soil.

The day began to heat as the sun rose higher. Mist came out of the ground and softened the look of things. Prickly Pear became green islands in a chalky sea. Mesquite groves took on the appearance of timber walls until you rode closer. His pony shied.

"Whoa, now. We're okay." He kept his voice low, calming the horse as he'd done a thousand times. Maybe two thousand. Then there was crashing in the brush off to his right and a longhorn steer ran past them, out of the mist into sight and then into the mist again. It carried a double R brand on its flank.

"Well," he said aloud, "I reckon we have arrived."

By the time he located the ranch headquarters all of the hints of fall had vanished. The sun was overhead in a blue sky, the mist had disappeared, and Harvey and his pony were both sweating. It was a working ranch, all right, not the kind of playpretty kept by some. The pole corrals were slick and shiny with use, feed cribs hung a little off plumb. The ground was hard. Out behind the main house wood smoke lifted off the tin roof of a log building. The smell of cooking was in the air. He rode toward it and saw three horses tied off in some shade trees, saddles still on.

Conversation halted when he came in the door. Three riders sat side by side on a bench at one of the tables. He could smell fried meat and he felt starved. A fourth man was bent over a stove down at the end.

Harvey took off his hat. "Good day."

The men were bare headed, their hats on pegs beside the door he'd just come in. Their hair was plastered down with sweat and rain and a morning of work. They belonged to the horses outside.

He thought it would be a good idea to talk to Raines first before he located the hired man. A courtesy.

"I'm looking for Mister Raines," he said.

One of the men stood up. "He ain't here; down in San Antone I think. Looking for a job?"

Harvey told him, "No, I really just need to talk to one of the ranch hands here. Name's Luther Welty."

The man grinned. "Luther ain't here right now, either. But he ain't far. You hungry?"

Two more came in before Harvey finished the meal. Fried beef with gravy and sourdough biscuits. The kind of grub you found all over the cow country out here. The five cowboys and the cook laughed and joked like they do, like Harvey had done as a younger man, and tried to find out all they could from him.

It wasn't much. Harvey was used to keeping himself to himself. He did admit to wanting a few more answers from Welty, things the deputy sheriff from Uvalde hadn't asked. He left them the impression, without saying so, that he was just another lawman with some questions.

"Looks like you law people would leave old Luther alone." The friendly fellow with the grin had turned serious. "He never hurt that whore. Sure, he liked to go have some fun with her, but so did we all. I guess every one of us has been there with her more than once. She was a pretty girl and everybody liked her, all right. But that's the kind of thing happens to whores. Am I right?"

Harvey put down his fork and said, "You were going to tell me where I can find Luther Welty." A low hum was building in his head. That happened sometimes. It had happened when he knocked Fisher Greene down the stairs three years before. It happened often when he pulled his Colt and took care of ugly business. He figured it might be best to leave before somebody crossed the line with their talk.

The cowboy read Harvey's face and looked away. "He went over on the creek. Got him a bad tooth."

"What?" Harvey sat silent, waiting for some kind of explanation.

"Indian feller down there. Medicine man or something. I ain't never been to see him, but some have."

From the other table one of the hands said, "He's helped me before. Pulled a tooth one time. Saved me a trip upriver. I'm the one told Luther go see him."

Harvey swallowed the last of his coffee. "Where'll I find him?"

"There's a creek goes into the river maybe a mile upstream. You likely forded it coming in." And yes, he remembered crossing a narrow tongue of shallow water back in the mist. He nodded. The man went on. "Anyway, you cross it and turn east and follow it a ways. Lives in a little shack affair right on the bank. You'll see it. I'd hurry on now, though, you want to catch Luther sober. The little man'll dose him good with mescal. I recall it as the best part of my treatment."

CHAPTER 15

Harvey thought the cabin merited a better description than the wranglers at the Double R had given him. Not a shack. Well-built and sturdy looking. Peeled cedar logs squared off like the German settlers did it, some kind of mortar packed in and smoothed off between logs. A skinny porch in front with a door of milled lumber and over it all a roof of split cedar shingles. Somebody had put in some work on the place. Off to the side was something built of poles and wire—a chicken coop. He saw a few of the birds walking around inside it. And next to that a fenced garden and a pole shed.

In an open copse of oak and elm at the cabin's front a haltered gray nibbled at grass. The horse carried the Double R burn. A dog stood in front of the porch barking at him as he rode up. A big dog. Probably three feet tall with long white hair. Harvey brought his pony to a stop and waited.

Nor, he decided, could the man who came out the door be called *little*. He was taller, in fact, than Harvey. Dark face, sharp as the blade of an axe. Hair in two braids down past his shoulders. He wore the same clothes as everybody else, but he was an Indian, all right. He said something to the dog. The animal stopped barking and went to a corner of the cabin and lay down.

"He won't bother you now."

Harvey's legs felt stiff when he stepped down. Over half a day in the saddle would do that to you. "Sorry to bust in on you."

"No, no." The man smiled and his face looked softer—like a dull axe, maybe. "Always glad to see company."

"Well, I'm looking for a fellow named Luther Welty. I'm told he's here."

41

"Yes, Luther's in the house. What do you want with him? He's in some pretty bad pain." This man spoke better English than most of Harvey's acquaintances. Not the kind of talk you expected to come out of a face like that.

"Just need to ask him a few questions, that's all. About a...a killing back in Stampede."

"Let's see if he's up to it. Tie your horse and come on inside." Harvey led the pony into the shade and slipped the bit out of his mouth. A rein around a sapling would hold him well enough. The Double R horse noticed them and sent out a low greeting and went back to the grass.

The cabin was one good-sized room with everything a lone man needed to live day to day. It was well-kept and neat with a round rug on a wood floor. On the back wall hung an unframed painting. It looked like oil on canvas, such as hung in the capitol back in Austin. This one, though, was not of a puffed-up man with the self-satisfied look of power. Instead, a longhorn steer looked straight at you, standing in agarita bushes with red berries on them—summertime in these hills. It looked so real you could walk right into it and stand beside that old bovine.

A split-log table took up the center of the room, flanked by three chairs with cowhide bottoms and a bench along one side of it. On the bench sat a young man with a swollen face and a bottle of mescal. He drank half a glass of it in one swallow and made a face. "Damn, that's raw stuff." He looked at Harvey. "Deke here says you want to ask me something."

The liquor had leached into the air around them, an odor slick as liniment but yeasty, too, almost like sourdough makings.

"Yes, sir. If you're Luther Welty." The cowboy poured another shot and drank it. He didn't bother to answer. Welty was just a kid, really. Probably not yet twenty years old. "You was there the night my...the night Ella died. That right?"

Welty nodded in silence and looked miserable.

The Indian said, "Why don't you take a chair. My name's McDonald, by the way."

42

Harvey shook the man's hand and said, "Kitren. Pleased to meet you. I'll hurry this up. Hate to be an aggravation to a man in pain." This was a strange Indian, all right. Where would he get a name like *McDonald?*

Harvey scooted the chair up and set his hat on the table between them. Welty said, "I was there, all right, but she was fine when I left. I already told all that." Harvey lifted his badge out of his shirt pocket and put it beside the hat.

"I heard you was a regular with Ella. That right?"

The young man looked closer at the dull metal. "You a Texas Ranger?"

Harvey tipped his head toward the badge. It was answer enough.

"When I could afford it, yeah." Welty grinned with one side of his mouth. "I liked that girl. She liked me, too. Told me so many a time." The man's eyes looked near to shutting. His face was slack and his words slurred. "She was a pretty one, all right. Nobody prettier, even the new girl."

"All I want to know is did you see anybody, see anything might help me...help us...catch the one did it?"

Welty appeared to be thinking, or maybe sinking into sleep. He shook his head. "Like I said. When I left, she was just fine like always." His eyes fluttered. The Indian spoke up.

"Mister Kitren, He's nearly asleep. I need to get at that tooth while he can cooperate with me."

"Sure." Harvey scooted the chair back and stood. He took his hat from the table and dropped his badge back into his pocket.

"You're welcome to stay. I'll be through in a few minutes. Luther will likely sleep for an hour or two." He held a fist-sized iron contraption that looked dangerous.

"Obliged, but I'll go on. Not much point bothering the man any more." Harvey walked toward the door. "Nice place you got."

CHAPTER 16

His pony looked calm, resting on three feet, a hind leg bent toe-down and eyes half closed. Harvey felt tired and disappointed. He'd wasted the day and learned nothing. He stood in the sun, enjoying the warmth of it on his shoulders. Then he thought of Ella and how she'd never have the sun on her shoulder again, and the loss began to hurt again. He got out his makings and rolled a smoke. The big dog got up from his resting spot and watched. Not a sound out here except a mockingbird and a couple of groans from Welty loud enough to hear through the door. Harvey ran his tongue over his own mouthful of teeth and hoped this kind of thing stayed somebody else's trouble. Well, he still had to make the trip back to Stampede. The mockingbird stopped his song and flew off. A horse came out of the trees along the creek, just the way Harvey had arrived a little while ago. The horse carried a man in buckskin.

Cee Tims said, "I didn't expect to see you again today." He dismounted and took a short rope off the saddle. He led the animal to a shade tree and tied him there. Harvey dropped the last of his cigarette and ground it out with a boot heel. He watched Tims walk back.

"Deke inside?"

"Yeah. He's pulling a tooth." So these men knew each other.

"Aha. One of his skills. You leaving? Or waiting out here til the ordeal is over?"

Harvey reached for his tobacco sack and remembered he'd just put one out. "Yeah. Headed back to town."

"I was hoping to beg something to eat from the man. You see anything edible inside?"

This one had a funny way of putting things. Harvey didn't answer the question. Behind him he heard the door open and close.

"Hey, Cee. How you doing?" McDonald carried a bucket around the side of his cabin. The dog followed him. Harvey heard something splash into the creek. The two returned. "Come on in, Cee." He paused at the door still holding the bucket. The dog lay back down. "You, too, Mister Kitren, if you'd like. Luther is in a mescal coma and the blood is cleaned up." Harvey thought about the blacksmith waiting to shoe his pony and the evening supper at Morgan Bailey's table. But there was enough time for both if he didn't stay here too long. Besides, he was curious. He followed the buckskin shirt through the door.

Luther Welty snored on a blanket, stretched out on the floor. The smell of the mescal was thick in the room. McDonald came back and opened the door. "Let's leave it open for now. Air some of that agave stink out." The iron thing he'd used for the tooth was on a shelf beside Harvey. It had been washed and was not yet dry.

"I never saw one of these before."

McDonald looked over. "Called a key," he said. "Goes in, you lock it down and turn a key that lifts the tooth out. I think it goes back clear to the Roman empire. How about some coffee?" He opened a cabinet door and took out a big can. "I bought a can of it already ground in San Antonio not long ago. Let's have some."

Tims said, "Anything to go with it? I'm about starved."

McDonald laughed and reached back inside the cabinet. "How about some eggs and biscuits?"

Once the stove was heated it wasn't long before coffee was poured and the biscuits baking. Harvey carried his cup to the painting on the wall. He drank. It was weaker than he liked, but it was good enough.

"You do this, Mister McDonald?"

"Call me Deke. Everybody does. Short for Deacon, which I'm not and never was. My daddy was a preacher. Still is. He

45

made me an honorary official of his church at birth. And no, I don't paint. That's a gift from my friend Cee."

Tims said, "Don't be critical now." He sat down at the table and took off the coonskin cap. "I got enough of that in New York."

This news was surprising. Harvey had been curious, of course, about the man who'd come along with him this morning. An artist? He'd never have guessed it.

"Why, no. I don't see anything wrong with it. Just the opposite, really. I admire it."

"A man with good taste." The artist laughed.

Deke said to him, "You're looking for your painting stuff, I guess."

Tims said, "You bring it in out of the rain?" He finished the eggs. Deke nodded. Tims swallowed and said, "I was worried til I saw your tracks headed back this direction. I knew then my old friend had saved my bacon again."

"You shouldn't leave all that stuff out here overnight like that. Get it stole or washed away in a flood ."

"Ah, hell, who'd steal it? Most of the time even I don't want it. And how often does it rain? That easel and canvas, and the oils. It's an awkward carry on a horse. Back and forth to town."

"You know you're welcome to leave it here instead of under a tree." Deke took his cup to the stove and poured an inch of coffee. Harvey came back to the table and sat down.

The Indian said, "I don't think you need to worry about Luther, Ranger. Like many young men he enjoyed his whores but there's no meanness in him."

"No."

"Tell me it's not my business, but I wonder why you're looking into that murder. You people don't meddle in local affairs usually."

"Well, it's...I can't talk about it just now. It's personal, you could say." He felt a surge of heat in his face. He stood. "I'd better head back."

"My question offended you."

"No, I just...Thanks for your help. And the coffee."

46

Cee Tims said, "If you'll hold up a second I'll ride back with you."

That was the last thing Harvey wanted to hear.

CHAPTER 17

The man was a talker. Harvey tried not to encourage it. Didn't matter.

"...Since the war. Deke saved my life back then. Dug that lead ball out and stanched the bleeding. He was a better surgeon than the doctor he was supposed to assist."

"Where'd it happen? Maybe I'm the one shot you." So, he'd put out some encouragement after all.

"Oh, somewhere in Georgia. Below Atlanta. I never was clear on it."

"You with that Sherman bunch?"

"No, later, but we marched in their ashes, clear down to the gulf waters."

"Wasn't me, then. I was being miserable somewheres else."

"The fight was between Indians, mostly. The Cherokee were split, you know. Some fought for the confederacy and others like Deke, for the union. They put Deke in the medical corps and that's where he learned what he knows."

"Is he a doctor?"

"No. He talked about going to school after the war, but I guess it wasn't an easy thing for a half-breed Indian. I don't know. We've never discussed it."

The day had warmed and moisture hung in the air. Harvey felt sweat under his shirt and imagined that the buckskin affair Tims wore had to be uncomfortable. Shadows narrowed and stretched longer as the sun slid below the tops of trees and the light of the day took on the expectation of the coming sunset. They rode past the stand of oaks he'd sheltered under this morning. The hours had passed too fast and left him nothing for his effort.

"Daddy's a preacher, I heard him say."

"Oh, yes. God's Methodist messiah to the heathen. Well, that's not fair, really. I never met him. He married a Cherokee, Deke's mother. He lived among them. Walked with them on the Trail of Tears. Probably a better man than I am."

"I've heard about that. Moved the whole bunch up to the Indian Territory. They say folks died."

"All true. Not all of them went, some hid out and stayed, but most did. Deke was a baby and has no memory of it, but he made the journey."

They were close enough to town now Harvey felt like he could let his curiosity out. "So you two got to know each other in the war."

"We did. Kept in touch by letter. He wandered down here and claims to love the country. I ignored his first letter describing his life in Texas, but was seduced by the fourth and came at last for a visit. The New York critics don't like my work anyway. Little to lose."

"He's been there awhile, then."

"Yes, the Homestead Act afforded him with eighty acres of free land, five years to prove it up, minus the three he served the Union."

"Looks like he'd be a rock in the Double R's boot, sittin' on the creek like he is."

"They get along. Raines considers him their private doctor. And, as you just learned, Deke is a charismatic man."

Harvey's thought was, *I just learned that, did I? Wonder what the word means.*

CHAPTER 18

Supper was good. He was hungry, nothing to eat since his meal at the Double R. No light showed outside the windows. Dark had settled in and the night was cooling down. The men had washed their hands and faces in the shallow washbowl on the back porch, lathering and rinsing and throwing the used water out the screen door. Cee Tims was still talking, this time to Dave Mikeska, who was a kind of professional listener, Harvey supposed. The young woman he would never get to know sat near him and avoided his eyes.

Mikeska kept on eating while Tims talked, and midway through something the man in buckskin was saying, stood up and said, "I need to get to work. Thanks for supper, Morgan. It was real good, like always."

The old woman lowered her fork and said, "Farewell, Dave. Watch out for the card cheats and gun hawks. You need a new line of work."

When the man had gone she said, to nobody in particular, "This would be a better town if that place burned down. That one, and the other one, too."

Harvey wondered which other one she meant, but he didn't ask. He figured he already knew.

He'd already shucked his boots and turned back the bedcovers, feeling tired from the long ride and depressed because he just didn't know where to go with his questions. Much as he needed sleep it seemed like a waste of time when he had no leads and Ella's murder went unresolved and unavenged. He wanted a smoke and hated to stink up his room. The air outside would be cooling down, but not cold. There were chairs on the front porch. He rolled a cigarette and lit it and opened his door.

And she was standing there with her fist raised, about to knock on it. Katy Wallace.

"I was going out on the porch for a smoke."

"You mind if I come, too? Not for a smoke. I don't use it. Just...I wanted to say a couple of things."

Harvey knew, had known since the night before, that something unsaid and unacknowledged had been passing between them. The attraction he'd felt from the first sight of her, the strange way about her, the shyness. Dave Mikeska saying what he never finished saying. *There's things...*

"I'd be pleased with your company," he said.

The porch planks felt cold on his bare feet. The rocking chair under him creaked on the rock back, but not on the forward motion. Nobody else was outside except an occasional rider headed down the street, probably to Lou Campbell's.

Katy Wallace sat on a straight-back chair three or four paces away. He couldn't see her face in the dark, but he could imagine the look of it. He waited for what seemed a long time until she finally spoke. In her voice he heard a tangle of shyness and reluctance and just behind it a resolve to get it said. A stampede of words over a steep cliff.

"How I knew Ella, I was a whore, too, down there at Lou's."

He hadn't been braced for it, and it bit into him hard. Hard. He felt his heart turn over. He put the tobacco roll to his mouth and sucked it down and threw the last of it past the porch rail into the dirt yard.

"It's nothing I'm proud of, and it didn't last long before I...anyway, me and Ella talked sometimes and I know some things I don't believe anybody else does. There's been gossip, no facts for anybody to bite down on." She stopped talking. He stayed silent, holding his own thoughts up like a man lifting up his pants legs out of mud. Held them rigid and didn't think them. Held his breath.

"I think you ought to know."

"Yes, ma'am. I'd like to hear what you got."

"I knew I'd hear that in your voice when I said what I did."

"Hear what?" But he knew. He knew what she meant.

"Never mind. Ella loved somebody. There was a man here. I don't know who. She never told me. One of her customers, but he was more than that. He made her promises and she believed him. He was going to take her away. That was what she thought."

"How long?" His lips felt like rocks banging together.

"What?"

"How long was it going on. With this man?" It mattered to him because maybe he would finally know what had held her here.

"All I know is it went back before. Before she came from Uvalde. So I guess it had been a few years. She believed him. Believed he loved her."

He heard himself say, "What kind of man loves a woman and leaves her to whoredom?"

"I don't know, Mister Kitren." She sighed. "Well, I've told what I know. Maybe it will help you." Her chair's legs thumped against the wood floor. He heard her steps approach the door and hesitate before she opened it and went inside. He knew she wanted him to stop her, ask her to stay. He had nothing to say.

CHAPTER 19

Morning was a long time coming. He fought his way up from dreams three times with his heart banging and his breath loud and raspy. Each time he tried remembering the dream that had thrown him back to consciousness, but could not. Nothing but snatches of it, like grabbing the hem of a garment going past. And losing it. After the last episode he heard a clock strike five somewhere in the house. Morning was close. He got up from the bed feeling relieved to be done with it, dressed himself and went out the door carrying his cup, wishing he'd brought his canvas jacket along on this trip.

Harvey didn't know how early the cafe opened, but figured he ought to stay away from there, anyhow. For today, at least. The idea of facing Katy Wallace rubbed a raw spot in his chest. He walked down the edge of the street, out of yesterday's mud, all the way to the end, hoping Ed Caudel had his forge lit and the coffee pot boiling.

The smell of hay and horses and coffee was a comfort. Caudel stood alone backed up to his forge. The lantern light inside showed him sleepy-eyed and quiet.

"You ever sleep?" Harvey said.

"Not much. Have some coffee."

He filled the cup and waited for the grounds to settle. You could hear the horses moving around. Daylight wouldn't be along for another hour or two. Caudel said, "Your boy's got new shoes. I stayed last night and put 'em on him. So he's ready to go when you are."

The coffee was too hot. Felt like it blistered his tongue. The warmth did him good, though, working its way into the middle of him. He held the cup out. "I think this's all I'll take out of here today. He can rest and get fat on your feed." Truth was, he

53

had no plans for the day, didn't know where to turn next. He worked on the coffee, grateful to Caudel and the stable and the hot forge that warmed him this cold morning.

The two men from yesterday came inside next and the blacksmith walked with them into the back of the stable. Cold air elbowed its way in when the door opened again. He moved a step closer to the forge and looked to see who it was. Caesar Tims. No buckskins this morning. He wore a regular shirt with a coat over it. On his head the same coonskin cap. He saw Harvey and smiled, wide awake with the look of stored energy ready for the day.

"Riding out again?" he said. He found a cup on a corner shelf and helped himself to the coffee.

"No. I was up early and nowhere else to go."

"Too bad. I'd like your company." Cee drank from his cup and made a face. He came closer than Harvey liked a man to stand. The ranger moved a half step away.

"You back out to McDonald's?"

"To pick up my easel, yeah. The brushes and oils and a painting I've been working on. I can finish it today if the light's good You liked the one on Deke's wall. I have three others like it in my room. Be glad to show them to you sometime."

Harvey nodded without comment. This was a man would take up your time if you let him.

Ed Caudel showed and said, "I've got your horse saddled. Same as yesterday okay?"

"Why, yes. It's flattering to be anticipated. Much like a good New York restaurant, I think."

"What?" the bearded man said.

CHAPTER 20

Cee and the other two cleared out and nobody else had shown up yet. Caudel poured himself a little more coffee and stood there with it. "Ever get the don'ts?" he said.

Harvey smiled for the first time today. Smiles had become strangers to him since that letter from Lou Campbell. "The don'ts? All the time, yessir."

"I swear I don't want to hit a lick at a snake today."

"Well, you're the boss. Give yourself the day off why don't you."

"There's a thought, now. How about you? You gettin' done whatever you came for?"

"Some of it." And he was thinking now that Ed Caudel was somebody he hadn't talked to except for horse shoes and oats. A friendly man right square in the middle of the comings and goings of the town. Harvey showed his badge and put it back in his pocket.

"I'm lookin' into a murder happened here a few months back."

"The young woman." He used a kinder description than Harvey had listened to lately. And because of what this man said and the way he said it, Harvey added, "My sister."

"My god. I'm so sorry."

"I appreciate it. I'm just askin' around, you know, lookin' for anything might help find who it was did it."

"You might hear a lot of gossip. The circumstances, I mean, people had their ideas for a while, but I never came across more than just plain old rumor and spite."

"One thing I learned lately is talk she was mixed up with a man. Outside of...not connected with the work..."

Caudel looked away. "I understand. Well, that's been a kind of whisper in the gossip, all right. I never heard anybody say it was the truth. Just the usual thing, you know, somebody told something to somebody else, and didn't know where it started. For myself, I chalked it up to myth. Could be true, of course, but I don't know that it would help you if it was."

A man came in the door, slamming it behind him, rubbing his hands together. Harvey saw a flash of morning light before it shut. He dumped his coffee grounds in the forge. They burned in a flash of sparks. He said. "I'll run on. Thanks."

"Yeah, time to go after that snake, I guess."

"Oh, just one question. I want to talk to the preacher at that church around the corner. Amos something. You know where I can find him?"

"Amos Brace, you mean. Yes, I do. He lives west of here a couple of miles. Got a little place out there. Or you can catch him tonight at the church. Wednesday service."

"Maybe I'll do that. Save myself a ride."

"Hope you'll come. I'll be there, too. Never miss it."

A man afoot, a man used to a horse under him, can feel stranded on the earth, moving slower than he's accustomed. Nearly helpless. He'd meant to pass it by, but the smell of frying bacon reached out from the cafe and he followed it inside, wanting food, but for sure not wanting to look into the bruised face of pretty Katy. Pretty Katy that was a whore. Not now, she said, and not for long, but did a woman ever stop being that once she was?

Somebody he'd never seen before asked him what he wanted. A medium-sized man with brown hair and a mustache that reminded Harvey of his own. What he wanted was some of that bacon and five or six eggs scrambled in the grease and some biscuits and gravy. Pretty Katy wasn't there and she didn't show up. Harvey put his empty mess cup on the table beside his hat.

"Been down to the stable," he said, when the man noticed it.

He finished eating, drank the rest of his coffee and left feeling glad he missed her. Or maybe not glad. Hard to be sure anymore. From there he wandered toward the river, back down the road he came in on two days ago. The river was wider now, too wide to ford on foot without getting wet up to his knees. And no place either side of the ford that offered a better way. It smelled green down here, like life, the stink of life, the mess of it. The muddy, mossy mess of it.

And snug beside it on that little hill, behind the cemetery fence, death waited. Neat, painted over, tucked away, past pain or sorrow. He watched a leaf in the current of yesterday's rain spin by.

CHAPTER 21

Over supper that evening Dave Mikeska said to him, "I mentioned to Fisher you wanted to talk to him."

Harvey nodded and chewed his food.

"He just said he'd be there when you was ready. At the saloon, he meant, I guess."

The whole day had melted down and lost its shape. The hours had passed and Harvey had spent most of them in his rented room, cleaning the colt revolver, staring at the wall, hearing the old clock strike its hollow chords somewhere in the house.

Mikeska looked up from his plate again and said, "He'll be there tonight, you want to come."

"No, I'm headed somewheres else this evenin'." He was in clean clothes and still had the smell of soap on his skin. He remembered the shirts and pants on the floor of his room and said, "There's a laundry in town I heard."

The woman sitting beside him stirred. Rosa. Rosa something. He didn't remember hearing her say a word at the table yet. "I work there."

"Well, I looked for it today and never saw it."

"Oh, it's in the alley, over behind the general store." Harvey realized he had not yet paid the woman any attention at all. His senses in this room had been tuned to Katy Wallace. The others had been like furniture to him, just there to take up space. He had thought of Rosa as the Mexican Woman, without form or feature. Now he noticed that she wore a long, pretty dress of calico. The color reminded him of a piebald horse he once rode. And like the dress, Rosa was pretty. Not like Katy, nor as young as Katy. But pretty.

"I'll carry some stuff over there tomorrow."

She turned to look at him and said "If you leave it outside tonight I'll take it when I go." Her eyes were a brown so dark they were nearly black. Her face was pleasant enough. It contained neither sorrow nor joy. Age showed in the sag of her cheeks.

"Obliged, ma'am." Maybe he'd do that. Maybe not, for unclear reasons. He didn't care for favors. Favors put you in debt. Good turns, back and forth until you forgot who owed who, like little whirlpools at the edge of rivers round and round. It had been his habit to do for himself, relying on no one.

Caesar Tims said, "I brought the new painting in if anyone wants to see it after supper."

Rosa glanced at the artist and said, "Maybe another time. I'm going to church in a minute."

Harvey heard Katy Wallace say, "You've been a long time with that one, Cee. I want to come look." Her words felt like a bone in his throat. A rock in his stomach. He wanted loose from her, from whatever piece of himself had stuck to her. Jealous. Of a whore?

He said to the Mexican woman, "Mind if I walk over there with you?"

Getting around on foot had never been his preference. The early years of his life on trail drives had made him that way. Not as bad as some men. He'd known cowhands who'd climb aboard and spur a tired mount when instead a hundred paces on their own two feet would have got them where they intended to go. The war had interrupted all that. Almost three years of his life, day and night, spent with infantrymen like himself who'd rather be cavalry and got stuck instead with rifle and bayonet and marching. They marched down bad roads and through woods and fought battles and then marched back to their tents if they were lucky. Some of those battles, though, the Yankees routed them and sent them running for their lives. That made defeat feel like a holiday sometimes.

On Sundays they marched after chapel for generals to watch and admire. Or for whatever reason generals watched. And often they marched, it seemed to him, just to be marching.

CHAPTER 22

"How long are you with us?" She asked him. They'd nearly reached the lit-up church house. Three buggies sat in front of it and he could pick out the shape of horses tied at the rails beside the building.

Two kerosene lanterns hung, one on either side of the open door, and showed the way inside. "I don't know for sure. A bit longer. You know this preacher?"

"Know him? A little, I guess. He baptized me. In the river down there at the crossing. But he's a busy man, you know. I don't talk to him since that day."

Inside the door a man reached out and shook Harvey's hand. "Welcome," he said. The fellow that waited on him at the cafe this morning. He saw a head of white hair in the flicker of candles up at the front. Ed Caudel. Half the benches were full. Young boys and girls sat apart, out of the light far as they could get, picking at one another, some of them barefoot. It was warm inside, though. Smoke leaked out of the cast iron stove in the corner, carrying a burn to the eye and a sharpness into the nose. Something everybody was used to, encountered every day in any house blessed by fire.

A man stood and stepped up onto the platform Harvey had noticed the first time he'd come in here days before. Rosa scooted halfway down a bench, making room for him. He followed her, feeling a little embarrassed. It implied they were there together. He would've preferred sitting alone, or maybe down there by Caudel. But it'd be rude to do it now, hurt the woman's feelings maybe.

"That's him," Rosa whispered.

He was a tall man. Even without the platform he stood on, he'd have towered above the congregation. A narrow beard of

61

well-trimmed salt and pepper hung on his face. His hair was parted down the middle and combed to the sides, dark and grey, a mixture like his beard. He wore the plain clothes of a ranch hand or farmer.

Brace gazed at the small group of people sitting on their benches in near-darkness, no light but candle-flame and kerosene lamp that danced across faces and walls. He said, "Will you stand for prayer." They stood, Harvey thinking not about the prayer coming from the preacher up front, but of the years he'd sat with Ella in a bunch of kids like these, whispering to one another, legs too short to reach the floor, waiting for all the singing and talking to end so they could get outside and play.

The words, the same words he'd heard over and over again through the years of his early youth, ended at last and everybody sat back down with the noise of scraping boots and shoes and the sighs of exhaled breath. Harvey wondered if Ella had ever remembered how it had been. Remembered, and all the while living the worst kind of life.

When he looked toward the front again the preacher had sat down and two others stood on the platform. A man and woman. The man held an open book so they could both see the words of the hymn. They sang *The Old Rugged Cross*. How many times had he heard it? Sung it himself with the bellow of young lungs? It was more than a song to him—more like a picture book of memories. There was no organ or piano, no fiddle as he'd once seen at a revival. The couple didn't need help. They sang with clear, powerful voices, a pretty woman in the middle years of her life, the man well set up, clean-faced. Harvey was glad when the song ended.

CHAPTER 23

Amos Brace turned out to be not so much a preacher as a talker. He talked. Harvey didn't mean to listen, but he liked the way Brace talked. Plain words, plainly spoken, not the shout and whine that kept him away from such as this, and had for many a year. The man finished up leaving you feeling like you'd heard not threats but promises. The couple sang again and the blacksmith, Ed Caudel, stood up and said another prayer, a short one, and it was over. The kids ran out the door.

Rosa started to rise, then realized Harvey was still sitting. She said, "You want to talk to him?"

"Thought I'd just wait til the crowd thins. You go ahead."

"All right." He moved his legs so she could get past him. Caudel saw him.

"Mister Kitren. Glad you could come." He was alone, like Harvey. "Amos will help blow out the lights when he finishes shaking hands back there. I'll introduce the two of you if you want."

The singers walked past and Caudel said to them, "Tom, Pearl, you sure sounded fine tonight. This here's Mister Kitren come for a visit. Tom and Pearl Forsythe." The woman smiled and the man shook Harvey's hand with a weak grip that slid away. "Tom clerks at the general store." They moved on and the room emptied.

Caudel had snuffed the candles along the front wall when the preacher finished his hand shakes and shoulder pats, shut the front door and walked down the aisle. He stopped at the bench Harvey sat on. Caudel said, "Amos, this fellow came to visit tonight. He wants to talk to you."

Harvey picked out a flash of white teeth in the midst of the dark beard and figured it for a smile. "Amos Brace." He offered a hand.

"Kitren. Good to meet you, Reverend."

"No, no title for me, sir. Not Reverend, not Your Holiness, nor any of the rest of all that popish nonsense. I'm Amos. What you want?"

Harvey stood. He didn't like looking up at the other man. Caudel had finished blacking out the church except for one kerosene lamp at the back near the door. He called out, "I'll go on now."

Brace said, "Goodnight, Ed" and waited for Harvey to speak up.

"They tell me you folks tend to the cemetery across the river."

"We do, yes sir. It was bad run down, and when I got this church launched we voted to take it on. Yes, sir."

Harvey reached for his tobacco sack and remembered where he was. He let his arm drift back to his hip. The candles and lamps had trailed soot into the air when Caudel extinguished them, the scents of tallow and kerosene mixing with smoke from the stove.

"My sister's up there. I want to see to putting a cross on her grave. A marker of some kind. It's unmarked now, and the one beside her is, too." He could barely make out Brace's face in the shifting flicker of that one lamp.

"Yes, sir. I thought I recognized your name. Sister, you say?" He walked a couple of paces away. "I need to bank the coals in that stove. Go ahead with what you're saying."

Harvey came up close behind the tall man while he opened the side door and swung it back, then stuck an iron poker inside it. The smoke came thicker out the opening. Coals and unburnt wood scraped inside it.

"I'll pay for it if that's what it takes. The other woman, too. I think she may've been a friend to Ella."

64

"Another whore is what you're saying, Mister Kitren." The preacher straightened up and propped the poker against the stove. He was a half-head taller than Harvey.

"No, sir. I don't believe I said that."

"We had a vote on this a year ago. Don't put no crosses on the graves of whores nor allow others to do it either. I can't help you."

Harvey slowed his breathing, heard that low hum start up in his head. He remembered again why he'd quit church meetings long ago. "You won't allow me to mark my sister's grave?"

"I understand how you feel about it, but it's our rule. Voted on fair and square. We don't allow markers on unrepented sinner's graves."

Harvey started for the door, slowly. "Amos, I'll be seeing to it myself and you need to pass the word. Anybody tries to stop me will find trouble." He opened the door and felt cold air on his face. "I rate you a good preacher but a sorry man."

CHAPTER 24

He forgot to leave his dirty clothes in the hall, so first thing come morning he rolled up shirt and pants and the rest and carried it all down the street and around the back to the laundry. A bell on the door jingled when he closed it. The air inside bloomed with the smells of wood smoke and hot water and felt damp on his skin. A man came from out of the back. The one who'd offered him stewed possum down at the cafe.

"I had you figured for a cafe man," Harvey said, and laid his bundle on the counter.

The man laughed and brought out a pad of paper and a pencil. "I'm a little of everything lately seems like. No, my wife runs the cafe. She's been sick for a while and I take up the slack when I can." He reminded Harvey of Ed Caudel, soft spoken and friendly.

"Sorry about your wife."

"Yeah, thanks. She's better now. I think she'll be back to work before long. You just want this washed and ironed?"

"That ought to do it. Rosa was gonna bring 'em over, but I forgot to leave 'em out for her."

"Oh, I guess you've got a room at Morgan's."

Harvey nodded.

"I've considered taking a room over there myself just for the cooking. Name, please, sir?"

"Kitren. Harvey Kitren." He watched the laundryman write it down.

"Rosa's in the back if you wanted to say anything to her." He scooped the clothes into a sack hanging behind the counter.

"No. No, thanks. I imagine I'll see her tonight."

"We appreciate your business, Mister Kitren. Your stuff'll be ready for you in a couple of days. Sooner if you need it."

Outside again, walking on the dirt of the alley, he noted the sun just up in a clear sky. The day would warm. Behind him, the bell from the laundry door and a woman's voice.

"Mister Kitren." Rosa.

He waited and she caught up with him. She carried a garment of some sort. Long sleeves hung down from it. Like a misshaped man with no life in him.

"I noticed you didn't wear a coat last night."

"No, I rode off without it. Thought I'd just buy me another one if it gets any colder."

"Here, then. It'll fit you, I think." It was a canvas coat with a flannel lining. The sort of thing he'd worn many a winter day. "It's okay. Been back there for a year now. Man left it for washing and never came back to get it."

Harvey took it from her. It looked all right. Had a little tear beside the right pocket, likely from a thorn. "You sure? I don't want to steal a man's coat from him." He slipped it on. She was right. It fit him well. It smelled clean.

"No, you go on and wear it. He was a stranger in a hurry. Been a year. He won't be back." She turned away.

He said, "Rosa?" She kept walking, glanced over her shoulder. "Thanks." She waved and went inside.

CHAPTER 25

He had a long day planned, and it wouldn't do to start out with an empty belly. Katy Wallace was waiting tables this morning. He could see her through the front window. Slow to make up his mind, he'd almost decided to go on when she looked through the window at him. He couldn't walk off now. No point hurting the girl's feelings.

She was friendly enough when she got his order and still friendly when she brought the eggs and sausage and biscuits. "I'll get your coffee in a second." The air around him was thick with the smell of food and grease, tobacco smoke and wood smoke. Katy seemed like she always did, like nothing had passed between them. Well, maybe it hadn't. Maybe the feelings and the conflict were inside his own head and nowhere else. Then here she was again, putting the cup in front of him and talking all the while to somebody across the room and walking off.

He was halfway finished when two men came off the sidewalk and took a table at the front. He heard them both ask for coffee and watched them as they watched Katy hurry off to the kitchen. The jealous feeling he didn't want to feel wrapped itself around his throat and made it hard to swallow. They kept their hats on, like they were in a hurry to finish and leave. One was a stranger to Harvey, a dark man, maybe Mexican, hard to tell. But for sure a man who spent his days outside under the sun. He wore range clothes, with dusty boots on his feet. His right pants leg was wet, like he'd just come across the river. On the left side of his face a scar, lighter than the skin around it, slid off his cheek and disappeared into his close-trimmed beard.

The other fellow wore town clothes, the sort of pants and shirt you saw on store clerks and gamblers. He had on shiny black shoes with a black string tie at his throat and a brown derby on his head. He was close-shaved, a handsome man, well set up, even if he had added some weight since Harvey last encountered him. Fisher Greene.

Katy brought their coffee and stood at the table in conversation he couldn't hear. She and Greene knew each other—that was plain. When she left the table Greene's eyes followed her figure until they swept past Harvey's face and then came back to him. Harvey swallowed the last of his food and the last of his coffee and let himself go still.

Greene looked as if he was thinking it over, never turning loose of Harvey's stare, and then he stood up and used a leg to push his chair back. The other fellow at the table was surprised by the sudden move, looked up at Greene and then at Harvey. The big man was an arm's length away in half a dozen strides. Harvey felt his heart hammer a couple of times, then quiet down as it always did when he faced trouble. He rose to his feet and pushed the chair under the table then took a step back. "Fisher."

Talk in the room had stopped. Even the kitchen clatter ceased. A man and woman got up from their table and went out the door.

"I hear you been lookin' for me." The voice hadn't changed. It seemed to carry threats no matter what words were used.

"I have been, yes."

"I see you got a weapon. I ain't armed."

"Well, you don't need to be. It's far too early in the day for such as that."

"Anyway, here I am. State your business."

His business wasn't anything he wanted to lay out in front of other people. Not in front of Katy Wallace, that was certain, but the circumstance didn't leave him much choice. "The last time I was here, on the stairs, it was wrong of me, what I did."

"You damned near beat me to death, Kitren. You saying you was wrong?"

69

"I'm offering my apology. I regret it."

"I hope sincerely you ain't got an expectation of a hug nor a kiss on the cheek. Cause you won't be gettin' such from me."

"No, I got no expectation. It's just, I been wantin' to express it, and now I have."

Greene's voice trailed down to a near-whisper. "I spit on your regret, Kitren."

Harvey nodded and picked up his hat. "Suit yourself."

The room stayed silent while he paid Katy for his breakfast. She tried a smile that didn't quite work when she took his money. He felt a tremor in her fingers and knew she'd been scared of what might happen just now. He was always surprised the way other people reacted when danger came. For him it had been the other way all his life. An all-over calm opened up inside him like a gift. A present he'd never questioned and no longer thought about.

CHAPTER 26

The colored woman said, "You'll have to ask Miss Lou about that. I may have knowed it, but can't remember if I did."

"I guess she's still asleep." Harvey's pony dozed at the rail out front. He was trying for an early start.

"You know she is." She smiled like they had a secret between them.

"Would you wake her up and ask her?"

"She liable to come up shootin'."

He dug in his pocket and held up a silver dollar.

She stared at it a second and blew a long sigh through her nose. "You got two them?"

"No. How about I owe you one."

"Wait right here."

Seemed like she was gone a long time, but it was partly due to his own impatience. No sounds in the big house, none from outside. Slow start everywhere this morning. He thought about Fisher Greene, a man who was bound to hold that grudge. And with good reason. Harvey had punished him bad, but it had been a bad time all around and Greene ought to've stayed out of it.

He heard footsteps on the stairs and the maid was back with a note in her hand. She grinned as she handed it to him. "I was you, I wouldn't come back around for a day or two. That woman treasure her sleep."

He rode for Uvalde and didn't return til near dark. He felt tired of the saddle and his pony was lax and slow in his movements coming up from the river crossing. The pony's ears perked when they were close to Ed Caudel's stable, thoughts of oats and corn no doubt coming to mind. Caudel was busy with another of his customers. A young boy Harvey hadn't met

71

before offered to unsaddle for him. A helper, he supposed, a boy of fifteen or so, who spoke with a heavy Mexican accent and in a shy manner.

"You work for Ed?"

"Si, yes. Sometimes."

"What's your name, son?"

"Manuel."

He found a couple of dimes in his pants pocket and held them out to Manuel. "Here you go, son. It's all I got on me. Yeah, unsaddle him and rub him down good, will you? Put it on my bill."

He slung the saddlebag over his shoulder and started for the street. Ed Caudel saw him leaving and called. "Mister Kitren. Hold up a second." He finished with his customer, shook hands with the man and caught up with Harvey.

"I'm curious to know if you and Amos got your business squared off last night. I hope so, anyhow."

"No, though I appreciate the introduction."

"I hate hearin' that. Is there anything I can do for you, on a personal level? I know you're in the middle of a hurtful time. And just say whoa if I push too hard."

"Good of you to offer, but no. I'll see to it myself. And next time you see me, call me Harvey, will you? I'm tired of *mister*."

CHAPTER 27

The two water buckets on the back porch were almost empty. He carried them out the screen door and poured what remained on the ground, then started for the well. He heard the creak of the pulley first, then realized somebody else was hauling on the well rope. He remembered Morgan Bailey's caution that some of the town people paid her for water.

The woman nearly lost her hold on the well bucket, startled at his footsteps. She sucked in a quick breath, then laughed. "I thought I was alone." She finished pouring and held the rope out to Harvey. The woman from church. The singer.

"No hurry, ma'am. My name's Kitren. Met you last night over at the church." He could see that she remembered him. "Sorry to say I forgot your name, but I thought you and your husband sung a fine hymn."

"Thank you, sir. We do what we can to serve the Lord." She began leaving, but her long dress caught on something. A splinter in one of the posts. She had to put down her water bucket and use both hands to free herself.

"And what is your name again, if you don't mind? I'll try to remember it next time."

She brushed at her dress and lifted the bucket again. "Forsythe," she said. He watched her carry her load out of sight. To the general store, he supposed. Ed Caudel had said her husband clerked there. Lending a hand tonight it looked like. She was somewhere in her thirties, maybe forty. A handsome woman, as people would say. But proper and pious and cold as a toad.

He carried the full water buckets inside and washed his face and hands, soaping and rinsing his skin clean, then blotting the water away with the fresh towel hanging there.

Morgan Bailey was in the kitchen where it seemed she mostly lived, filling bowls and getting plates out of cabinets. "You're my hero," she said. "A fine boy. Thanks for the water." He passed Katy Wallace in the hall. On her way to help with supper. He offered a silent nod. She didn't notice it because her own eyes were focused on her shoes.

In his room he wiped his colt revolver clean and checked the loads, then put it away, trying not to wonder about the feelings he'd carried inside from the hall. Harvey was a practical man, always had been. That girl—Katy—was not for him. Couldn't be. She was what she was. A soiled woman, plain and simple. Living in a proper manner now, maybe, but it was a stain, a vein of coal through her system, inside her spirit. Not something he could overlook. And from there his thoughts jumped to Ella, his sister. Not long ago he'd argued with her, pled with her, to leave this place and the life she led.

What was it he'd wanted? Why, to come with him, of course, go back to the right kind of life. And if she had...if she had...if she had done what he wanted, would he have found a way to forgive her, let her back into his life and forgive the past? Seen her again clean and washed and deserving?

Thinking about it felt like a handful of sand in his head, gritty and shifting. Maybe Ella knew better than he did. Maybe she understood that her stain was a permanent thing that could never be washed or talked away. What he had believed that day was that the stain could be forgiven. And that forgiveness might somehow cause it to disappear. Somebody knocked on his door.

Dave Mikeska. The man stood in Harvey's open door looking uncertain. He may have expected Harvey to ask him inside. "Evenin' Dave. I was about to go to supper."

"Well, sure. I'm ready myself." He paused, then said, "I was just by the saloon a few minutes ago. Heard some talk I wanted to pass on to you personal."

"Come on in, then."

Mikeska walked in and Harvey shut the door behind him.

"Fisher is crowin' about a run-in with you this mornin'. Sayin' he backed you down." Silence then, like he was waiting for affirmation or denial. Harvey said nothing.

"He's wearin' his gun now, says he was unarmed this mornin' and expects to kill you next meetin'. Thought you ought to know."

"Thanks, Dave. I appreciate it. But don't worry. I'll be fine, and expect he will be, too. Let's go eat."

CHAPTER 28

The meal was tasty. No surprise there. Cee Tims had been off somewhere all day painting another picture. The man needed appreciation, that was clear. He said to Rosa, who sat beside Harvey again, "You missed my exhibition last night. Mister Kitren did, too. I insist you come see my work tonight after supper."

"Of course I will, Cee." She drank from a glass of water. "I can't speak for this man, though."

"Be happy to," Harvey said.

The room was crowded with all sorts of stuff that Tims must have carried in from his jaunts. Pieces of driftwood from the river. Rocks. The buckskin costume he'd worn the day of the big rain. The coonskin cap on a hook beside the door. You could smell the oil paint that decorated what appeared to be at least a dozen canvases leaning against a wall. And the scent of turpentine in the close air. An easel stood beside the only window holding what must have been an unfinished painting. Some image Harvey couldn't identify was blocked on it with dark markings.

Rosa had come along with him. Mikeska had left for work and the other two women were clearing the dinner table. Morgan Bailey had said, "We saw it last night. And besides, nobody can really appreciate an artist anyway, til they're dead you know."

Cee laid five canvases across his unmade bed and stood back waiting for whatever it was he needed to hear. Harvey liked them all, and said so. They were all similar to the one he'd seen hanging on Deke McDonald's wall. Cattle and the range they lived on. Cactus and thorny brush. Riders on tired horses.

Rosa said, "You're a very talented man, Cee." Harvey figured that was what the artist was waiting to hear. It brought out a shiny smile.

"Kind words. Thank you. I hope the critics back east feel the same."

"You're headed back there, then." Harvey.

"Well, yes, that's always been my intent. There's a gallery in New York that will show the work."

Rosa said, "I have things to do. I wish you success, Cee. Good night, all."

Harvey stayed where he was. He'd never attached himself to circumstance or situation, always made it a point to keep a distance between himself and other people. But Caesar Tims raised curiosity in him. A man of brash behavior and unquestioned talent camped here in a little town above the Chihuahua desert. Harvey felt no closer to finding Ella's killer than the day he rode into Stampede. And in truth he had begun to wonder if there was any chance of finding justice for Ella.

He hadn't talked to nearly enough people, hadn't asked nearly enough questions. Time was slipping past.

"I was wondering," he said, "how you came by your interest in scenes like these. The land, the stock that run on these ranges. Seems to me the sort of thing a Yankee like yourself would find beneath him. I mean no offense."

"A Yankee, eh? Well, don't worry, I don't find it offensive. But I don't consider myself a Yankee. I fought on the Union side in the war because I believed it was the side of right. No, I am a citizen of the world. I've sailed to Europe, to England, studied painting in Paris. Spent untold hours in the Louvre."

"Won't surprise you to know I got no idea what you're talkin' about."

"The Louvre is home to the greatest art collection in the world."

Harvey rolled a smoke and lit it. He offered the sack to Cee Tims.

"Thanks. I don't use it." He wasn't finished. "My family came here from England. My grandfather was descended from nobility. He was a painter, too, and quite successful. I suppose I inherited his ability. His name, though, was Thames." He spelled it for Harvey. "Since it is pronounced as Tims, my father changed the spelling. We are named for London's river."

"So you came to visit your friend, Deke? Decided to stay on a while and turn out some painting?"

"That sums it up, yes."

"And pretty soon now you'll take all these pictures back east and show 'em what things are like out here. I like what you've done. How about them over in the corner? More steers? I didn't look at them."

"Uh, no. Those are portraits. People who interest me. Most are quick sketches."

"Can I see?" Harvey was already moving across the room. He transferred the smoke into his left hand and used his right hand to raise the outside canvas into the shifting lamplight. A woman's face stared back at him. It was an incomplete face, a line here, a line there, shades of color that barely showed, but you couldn't miss who it was. Lou Campbell. Only one man in the whole pile and it stood out—Fisher Greene.

Then another woman, and another, just their faces. Katy Wallace was in the stack, sad-eyed and the look of loneliness easy to pick up. Then, what he'd feared, Ella's face came up from the shadow like some angel. All innocence and smile. All heartbreak.

He put them back.

"That portrait of your sister is yours if you want it. A gift."

"Well," Harvey's face felt hot. He had no memory of telling Cee about himself or about Ella. No doubt word had spread of the mission he was on. He pinched out the cigarette and held it in the palm of his hand, ignoring the burn in his thumb and finger. "Maybe I'll take it with me when I leave town. Obliged to you." He had more questions now, but his thoughts emptied out. He failed to locate any words to be used in conversation. "I better go on now."

"Of course. Thanks for coming."

When Harvey swung the door open to leave, the buckskin costume that hung on the back of it lifted in the rush of air and brushed at his shoulder as if bidding him a good night..

CHAPTER 29

A kerosene lamp and two candles lit the kitchen. Katy Wallace was in the room alone, drying the last of the supper dishes. He thought she must be the hardest working woman he'd ever known.

He was tired from the long ride to Uvalde, but the sight of Ella's face in that portrait had put a knot in his chest and made him dread sleep. The dreams that might come with sleep, anyway. He put his hand to the stove, felt a rush of heat and jerked it back. "Still hot," he said. "Can I borrow a candle?"

"Sure you can. Going after water?"

"Thought I would, yes." Maybe a tub full of hot water in that little shed out back would ease the hurt he was feeling tonight. He drew one bucket and left the candle burning at the well while he carried it inside. Katie had put the big kettle out for him.

"Read my mind, I guess."

"Yes." She was almost finished with the drying chore.

He wished Morgan Bailey would come back to the kitchen. He felt clumsy with Katy, foolish and wanting in common sense. "I'll bring in more water if you want to heat some for yourself."

"You taking a bath outside? In the shed?"

"Thought I would."

"It would be good of you to bring in full buckets when you're done. Save Morgan a trip to the well in the morning."

"I'll be sure to do that." He listened for the sound of steam from the kettle, but heard none. Through the back window he could see the far flicker of the candle where he'd left it beside the well. Katy had turned away from her dishpans now and stood watching him, making no move to leave the room.

"You don't have to hide from me," she said. Her face was neutral, without a smile or a frown. She seemed at ease.

"What?"

"I don't ask your approval of me, of my life, but I'd appreciate a kind word now and then."

"Well, ma'am, I didn't realize I'd showed unkindness." That was a lie, he knew, but what else could he say?

"That was surprising today, what you said to Fisher. Men like you don't offer up regrets that often."

"Well..." He tested the kettle again, wishing it would boil. There was nothing else he could say, nothing to be done about this awkward confrontation. He felt his heart beat in his throat.

"One time," she said.

"Pardon?"

"One time. One drunk cowhand. A half a dollar. That was the start and the finish of it."

"Don't guess I know what you're referrin' to, Miss Wallace."

"Yes, you do." And she just kept on looking at him. That was the worst of it, because he couldn't meet her eyes. Something was building in him, like storm clouds at the horizon, hot clouds carrying shame instead of rain. He grabbed the kettle off the stove and headed out the door.

CHAPTER 30

The tub of water was lukewarm, not nearly as hot as he would have liked, but it felt good, anyhow. Good to be alone in the shed with the door latched and the candle from the kitchen throwing shadows against the wall. Good to be out from under the weight of Katy Wallace's eyes. She'd sent him running, all right. Couldn't be denied. Had to hand it to her. Honest and straight up. *One time. A half a dollar.* It seemed to him just then that the stain he'd been seeing in her had turned into a smudge. Something that might be just wiped away by a caring hand. Or a kind word.

He'd brought no towel, rushed as he'd been. He stood dripping in the new cold of early night, all goosebumps and shivers, then got into his shirt and pants, their cloth sopping the water off his skin. He decided to carry his boots and walk back inside barefoot. He reached for the candle with his free hand. As he lifted it off the shelf the movement caused its flame to double in size and in the light something flickered. Something on the near wall. But he saw nothing there. He moved the light closer. There. Not on the wall, but inside it, a thin reflection. It was metal, a few inches long, in a crack between boards.

The knife was the sort of thing you saw in a woman's kitchen. A thin wooden handle bradded onto a blade of hand-length metal. The blade was honed down from use and appeared to be rusted like it had been stuck up there a long stretch of time. But no, he scraped it with a thumbnail and realized the stain was something else. Blood? Old and dried. The shock of it caused him to nearly drop the thing. No way to know for sure. Maybe somebody had used it to butcher meat. One of Cee's deer? Or maybe somebody had used it for a darker purpose.

The house was quiet, nobody else stirring. Harvey left the knife in his saddlebag, certain in his soul it was Ella's blood on the blade. He got his feet dried and his boots back on and went after the water he'd promised.

Sleep came and went all night long, questions running through his mind like mice. Somebody here in this house? One of these people he ate supper with? Those paintings of Caesar Tims meant he'd spent time with the women a few houses down. Spent time with Ella. Enough time to spread her looks on canvas with a brush. Maybe there was more to it than that. Cee had painted some of the others, though. Not just Ella. But still...

He felt used up when daylight came. Heavy and slow. He wanted the thoughts and the questions to let up, wanted peace in his mind and his heart. He got the knife out again and looked it over, wondering where to go next. He carried it to the kitchen.

Morgan Bailey was already at work, snapping peas, getting ready for a supper that was twelve hours away. He thought he might understand why she was that way—an old woman alone with a houseful of strangers; constant work, never-ending movement necessary to keep the silence out of her head. He'd wrapped the knife in a bandanna. No need to leave it in the open for any prying eye.

"You bring the water in last night?" She glanced up from her chore.

"Yes, ma'am, I did." He remembered he had not gone back to empty the number two tub he'd washed in.

"My arthritic bones thank you, then."

He unwrapped the bandanna and held out the knife. "You recognize this? One of yours, maybe?"

She straightened her back quickly and took in a deep breath, startled at the sight he'd put in front of her. "Why, I don't know. Where'd it come from?"

"I found it last night. Stuck in a crack inside your shed."

"Something on the blade."

"Blood, I think. Has anybody done butchering back there? I know Cee brought a deer in."

"Not that I know of. Cee dressed that buck out at his friend's place. And no, now that I look closer at it, it's not one of mine. I wonder how on Earth it got out there."

"I'm wondering the same thing." Harvey took his Ranger badge out and showed it to her. "Keep quiet about it, please, ma'am, til I can figure out how to proceed."

She smiled. "Of course I will. And you can put that tin thing back in your pocket. Everybody in town knows who you are and what you're doing here."

CHAPTER 31

He wandered down to the cafe for some eggs and coffee. Katy waited on him, polite as always, none of the look in her eyes left over from last night. It was nearly funny if you thought about it. Like some barefoot schoolboy. Liking a girl, getting all wobbly-kneed around her, afraid to step up and say so. And she'd seen it in him, hadn't she. She knew, and him all along thinking his secret thoughts. Smart girl. He finished the second biscuit and the last bite of fried egg and followed it with the last of the coffee. He rolled a smoke and watched people walking past the window, listened to the ragged edges of other people's conversations, kept his eyes off the moving figure of Katy Wallace while somehow noting every step she took.

She came to the table and asked if he wanted more coffee.

"I saw your picture with some others last night. Looked like Cee spent time down at Lou's place. That where you posed for him?"

"First time you came in here I thought I saw something appealing in your face and manner. That's no longer the case, so here's some advice. If you can't be kind, at least show some respect. A little politeness, if you can. No. He sketched me with a piece of charcoal sitting at the supper table where you eat at night. Coffee or not?"

Well, the words had just popped out. He hadn't meant to insult her. There was something...something he'd seen or heard—what was it? Couldn't remember, or maybe never knew. But it was still in his head, if he could only find it. It had jarred him a little, left an impression, then flown on past and now he couldn't get hold of it.

"Uh, no, I believe not. Sorry if I offended you, Katy. It was not my intent."

She made an about face and without word or gesture went off across the cafe to tend to somebody else. Harvey left money on the table and walked out to the street carrying his hat in one hand. He had time to wonder what he ought to do with the day ahead before a whiplash of sound split the morning and a lead slug ripped its way through his scalp, tore across the bone of his skull and embedded itself in the wall behind him.

CHAPTER 32

Harvey's world came down to a tunnel of light surrounded by darkness. He went to his knees on the boardwalk then slammed into it face-first, his hat flying out of his hand into the street, his half-finished smoke beside it, snuffed out in the sand. The bullet had failed to knock him senseless. He knew what had happened, could hear screams and loud voices, felt the touch of hands and the heat of blood on his face. He wondered how bad he'd been hit, and then he slid over the edge of something and floated downward in darkness.

When he came back to the world he showed up all at once. No slow drift back to consciousness such as he'd experienced a time or two in his life. First thing was the breath of somebody on his forehead. A face close to his, looking down at him. A burn across the top of his head, the smell of something harsh as lye. A poke and pull through the burning place. A headache that seemed to roll from one side of his head to the other. He opened his eyes.

"Back with us, are you?" The poke and pull never stopped. The words sounded offhanded, like the speaker was not surprised. It was a man's voice, and he'd heard it before but couldn't place it. No face to go with it, and the man was hunched so close as to appear a blur in Harvey's vision.

He tried to sit up.

"Ho, ho, whoa now. Stay down. Got to get you sewed back together." He was on his rented bed in his rented room. Familiar wallpaper and furniture around the bed.

"Didn't kill me." The words came out like a frog croak.

He heard a chuckle from above. "I hope you'll will your skull to science, Mister Kitren. It may be the hardest one

87

observed so far." The poking and pulling never stopped. Harvey remembered the voice.

"The laundry."

"Well, yes, that was me." Harvey could feel puffs from the man's breath as he talked. "I was helping out a friend that day."

"You a doctor?"

"I am today. Now be quiet and hold still. I'll have you done in just a minute."

Harvey did as he was told. He lay still, going over in his mind what had just happened. Somebody had ambushed him. Laid in wait across that street til he came out of the cafe and tried to put a bullet in his head. And it was a wonder it had not worked out that way. Had the shooter held a truer aim it would all be over now. The situation required a good deal of thought but that would have to wait. Just now, thinking was like that feeling you get rubbing two coins together, or two marbles in your hand. A kind of sliding, grating friction that made you want to stop.

He heard the snip of scissors and felt fingers probe at the repair. "That'll do it. How's your head feel?" The big man stood up and the mattress under Harvey shifted. He could see the familiar face now, a man he'd first believed a cafeman, then a laundryman, and knew now was the town doctor. A many-talented man, for sure.

"Not good." He moved his head and saw that there were others in the room—Morgan Bailey in a chair by the door, watching with a kind of quiet certainty. Katy Wallace standing beside her, one hand on the older woman's shoulder. The movement hurt.

"I can help you with it. Give you something to help you sleep. Far as I can see you're not bad hurt, although that bullet gave you a mighty slap. I think you ought to just stay down the rest of the day, sleep a while and let's see how you're doing in a few hours. Okay by you?"

"Who was it? Shot me? Anybody see?"

Katy spoke up. "Nobody knows. They were in the alley beside the general store. Somebody on a horse, and they rode out the back way, back this way, probably across the yard by the well. Morgan didn't see anybody, though."

"No," Morgan said, "but I went out and looked a little while ago and there are some fresh hoofprints, so I guess Katy's right."

The doctor said, "Morgan, would you get me a glass of water?" He pulled a bottle from his bag and took out two pills. "I cauterized the wound, so I don't expect it to bleed any more. Always amazes me how much a man can bleed out of his noggin. And I sterilized it well with carbolic acid. I imagine you're familiar with that concoction. These pills of mine will put you to sleep and tamp down what I imagine is a rip-roarer of a headache."

Katy Wallace came over to the bed and helped lift him shoulder high so he could swallow the pills. The movement caused the room to spin around a couple of times.

"You ought to wake up about supper time."

Harvey shook his head, which hurt again. "No. No pills. May want to try for me again."

Morgan Bailey said, "I won't let nobody come in here and hurt you."

"No, no pills."

"Well, then, suit yourself," the doctor said. He put the bottle back and zipped his bag shut. "You might want to take a couple of minutes to thank the good Lord. It's a miracle you are not a dead man."

CHAPTER 33

Somebody had tried waking him. He couldn't remember who, but he remembered telling them to just let him sleep. It had been his aim to remain alert in case there was another attempt to do him harm. But the sharp headache, the dizziness, the effects of the bullet wound, had worn him down. The room was dark. He'd finally come awake in the middle of the night. In fact it was Morgan Bailey's loud clock striking midnight that brought him up from a deep and dreamless sleep.

He wondered if he could stand and tried it to find out. He put his feet on the floor and stood up slowly, ready to sit back down if the room made that spin again. But no, except for the dull ache in his scalp and a sore nose where he'd hit the boardwalk, he felt pretty good. Not tops, but not bad. There was enough moonlight through the window he could see a glass of water on the bedstand some kind soul had left for him. He drank it dry and could have used more, but the walk to the kitchen didn't seem worth the trouble.

Cold in the room, but he felt comfortable. Took him a second to figure out how he came to be wearing a long flannel nightshirt over his underdrawers, and the memory of Caesar Tims and the old woman fussing at him, rolling him in the bed, pulling at his clothes, came back. He couldn't help smiling at that, and the tug of skin caused a new hurt on his right cheek. Probably had a bruised face, maybe a black eye.

His shirt and pants were folded over the back of the room's straight chair. He managed to locate the tobacco sack and found enough left for one, so he rolled and lit it and sat on the edge of the bed smoking, feeling wide-awake, wanting to get dressed, get some coffee, and get busy. Doing what, he was not certain.

First light took a long time arriving. He pulled on his boots and went out the door, glad again for the jacket Rosa had given him. The house was quiet, nobody else in the hallway.

The general store was open. The church singer, Forsythe, with a white apron on and a black string tie at his throat, sat behind a low table in a corner emptying out a shipping crate. A wood stove beside the table warmed the shop. Harvey smelled leather and raw beans and the oiled sawdust used to sweep the floor clean. The man looked fresh-scrubbed and shaved. The store was empty of customers. Forsythe looked up from his task when Harvey came inside.

"Morning, sir."

"Morning. You got a sack of Bull Durham I could buy?"

"That I do." He left the table and opened a glass-front cabinet and handed the tobacco to Harvey. The two yellow strings that held the sack closed were pinned under the label along with the orange pack of rolling papers that went with it. "Just got this in, so it ought to be good and fresh."

Harvey paid for it and said, "I told your wife I enjoyed your song at church the other night."

The man stared. "I just realized you're the fellow shot yesterday."

"Yeah. I have not looked in a mirror yet. What do you think?"

"You'll pass muster, all right. I guess the bullet wound's under your hat from what I've heard. That eye's got a purple look around it, but I'd say you was lucky to live over it."

Harvey freed up the papers and rolled a smoke. "You here in the store when it happened?"

"I was putting up some stock on a back shelf. I heard the shot through the wall, over in the alley by the store. Nearly jumped out of my shoes it was so loud."

"Didn't see anybody I guess."

"No, sir. I heard people yelling and ran outside, saw you on the ground. I'm the one went and got Doctor Pruett. They'd carried you over to Morgan's when I made it back here to the store."

"Well, I thank you for your effort." Harvey stuffed his new tobacco sack in a pocket and turned to leave.

"You need a set of spurs?"

"I guess that means you've got some to sell."

"I was just unloading that batch over by the table. Had 'em on order since August and they came in yesterday. Got a feller freights stuff down here from Uvalde. Stage won't come this way, shunts off and heads for San Antone. Makes it hard bringing merchandise in." He swung a casual hand. "Anyways, thought I'd ask. Got us a couple dozen sets now and they'll go pretty quick."

"Obliged, but I don't wear 'em. Tried it one time and it hurt my pony's feelings. We reached agreement on the subject." He left the man laughing.

CHAPTER 34

Harvey walked down the alley and around the dogleg that led into the back yard of the rooming house. And yes, even in the sparse early light he could see the sharp cut left by shod hooves moving fast. The prints continued past the yard and behind the two shacks that stood between Morgan Bailey's and the vacant lot beside the fence around Lou Campbell's. Through the lot and into the makeshift street, then who knew where.

He retraced his steps and saw his landlady walking toward the well carrying two buckets. She put them down beside the well and rubbed her hands as she watched him approach. She'd mentioned arthritis, probably took time to get moving on cold mornings.

"Let me help you."

"My hero. Good morning. I'm happy to see you on your feet."

"Yeah, I'm alright." He dropped the well bucket, heard it splash, waited while it filled and began hauling it back up. "Appreciate all the help last night." He transferred the water to one of her waiting buckets and drew another.

"Makes me catch my breath, how close you came. Hard head or not, one or two inches lower and we wouldn't be having this conversation."

"Yes, ma'am. Worries me some, too. Anyway, here's your water. Let me carry it in the house for you."

She held the door for him. He settled everything in place and realized he was thirsty. He took the tin dipper off it's nail and scooped up a dose of the fresh, cold water.

"You want some coffee?"

93

The old woman had a fire in the stove and a pot of some sort steaming.

"I thought you said supper only. Don't want to take more than I'm entitled to."

"You're a wounded hero. Take advantage of it."

"Sure, then, I would. What is that contraption?"

She opened a cabinet and took out a big white mug. "This was my husband's cup. Had his coffee out of it every morning. Don't drop it."

The handle was warm in his hand as he swallowed the hot brew.

She said, "This's a percolator. Fancy thing from England. Water heats up, goes up a sort of chimney and then drips back through the coffee. You miss grounds in your cup?"

"A little bit, I guess, but I'll get over it."

"The same husband whose cup you're holding, carefully I hope, was a freighter. Hauled stuff all over this country. He brought me the percolator one of his trips."

"Man at the store just now said everything comes in by wagon."

"Always has. Used to stop here and turn around, go back up to Uvalde then west. Now they go on south to Eagle Pass, right at the border. Man by the name of Braca took it over. Something about him never did smell right to me. Shifty. Friend of that whoremonger, too."

"Fisher Greene?"

"Yes. The very one. So you see what I mean."

He figured the odds were good that Greene had pulled the trigger on him. A long talk with the dandy was coming due. "Fisher was at the cafe with a man the other day. Dark fellow, looked Mexican to me. Had a scar on his face."

"That was him. Trey Braca. If you was not introduced you didn't miss a thing."

Harvey sipped at the coffee, enjoying the heat from the stove and the conversation with Morgan Bailey. The headache was about gone and he felt close to normal. The woman talked about the husband she'd lost to pneumonia six winters back.

94

Sounded like, with no children, she was alone in the world and making her way as best she could. Everybody has their own story, he thought to himself. And now and then need to tell it. Does no harm to listen, sometimes.

The talk wound down and the mug emptied. He felt sleepy and tired.

"Here, let me have that. You want another one?"

"Thank you, no. Believe I'll go doze a while."

"Gonna wear the nightshirt again?"

He smiled and shook his finger at her and went down the hall to his room.

CHAPTER 35

He dreamed deep dreams of his family; mother and father and Ella. When the knocking came on his door he fought waking up because it seemed to him if he could stay asleep then Ella would stay alive. To open his eyes was to let her die again.

A voice called to him. "Mister Kitren. You in there?"

And so he let it fade. Nothing could be done about it. The clock struck one just then. Afternoon already. He hadn't meant to sleep the day away. He swung his boots to the floor. He remembered meaning to take them off, but couldn't stay awake long enough to get it done. "Hold on. I'm coming."

The colored boy from the stonecutter in Uvalde stood in the hall. "Sorry. I was takin' a nap."

"Yes, sir. Well, I hate I woke you up, but Mister Osgood sent me after you. Said you need to come show us the place."

"Didn't expect him for a few days yet."

"Yes, sir. He just got right to it, and he's a quick worker."

"I need to get my horse. You can tell him I'll be there in a few minutes."

The old man and his helper stood over a small fire warming their hands when he rode up. The bay pony didn't want to stop. He was full of stored up energy and seemed to think they were headed back to Austin.

Harvey felt bad about Ed Caudel.

Caudel had said, with that white smile of his, "Where you off to today?"

So it had started, like he'd known it would, with him tempted to lie. But instead he'd replied, "Just up to the graveyard."

96

Caudel had nodded and turned serious. "Hard thing, I know. I lost a brother many years ago and it still hurts me to think about it."

Knowing he ought to mount up and ride off, Harvey said, instead, "I'm puttin' a marker on my sister's grave. Had it made in Uvalde. The man's here to set it down."

And Caudel had dropped his eyes to the ground then and found somethng to look at for a little while. "You'll get no argument from me."

"No sir, I didn't think so, and I'm glad of it. I've come to think highly of you."

"It's the women's the problem. And Amos, I'm sorry to say. I think the world of the man, but I never agreed with the vote they took."

"I better go on. They're waitin' on me."

"Just—they're good people, the church folks. I hope nobody gets hurt over it, that's all."

"Well, I aim to do what needs doing. I'll match force with force, like I told your preacher Brace."

Old man Osgood looked like a stretch of wire that could bend any which way and come back straight. His hat perched on the wagon seat in front of the two marble stones. They lay side by side with the chiseled letters in view.

Osgood said to the boy, his helper, "Put some water on this fire, Jasper. Still droughty out here. Things is dry"

Harvey found a sapling and tied the pony. He said, "You made it a quick job of it."

"Yes, sir, I did. But a good one. You won't find no fault with my workmanship."

He leaned over the side of the wagon and looked them over. They were made of rose-colored marble, shiny, Ella's reading *ELLA KITREN, BELOVED SISTER AND DAUGHTER*. Her birth and death dates showed her age at 36, with a carved scroll around it all. The other one read simply *MYRA DAVIS, SOMEONE'S DAUGHTER*. With the same scroll. The name Lou Campbell had written on the piece of paper. He remembered he owed Lou's maid a dollar.

"They look heavy," Harvey said. "I can help you with them."

"No need, sir. Me and Jasper is used to it."

It took them another hour to get it done, planting the stones deep enough so they wouldn't fall over. Harvey watched, feeling useless.

Osgood said, "Now, you want the little fence around both graves, together? Or each one separate? I brought enough either way."

"I don't know if they were friends. I don't know if they maybe even knew each other. But yes, sir. Together. Don't guess it means anything to them, but it means something to me, knowing she's not by herself out here. Fence 'em in together."

It stood six inches high, made of smooth wire that arched over and hooked together. Harvey thought it looked peaceful and private now, where she lay. And his love for her was cut into stone. No rain would wash it away.

He watched the wagon cross the Frio, then climb the road and go around the bend at the top. He smelled the wet smoke off the dead fire and wondered what to do next. Bound to be some reaction from Brace and the church people. But when? They didn't even know yet what he'd done. And he couldn't stand out here day and night guarding the graves. Truth was, he hadn't thought much past the disgust he felt at their attitude toward his sister.

Surely, though, they'd leave things as he'd just made them. If they were, as Ed Caudel had said, good people, they wouldn't begrudge a man offering up what he could to a sister forever gone.

No choice here. When he'd told Amos Brace the folly of interfering, he'd meant every word of it, and now he'd have to wait and find out if the threat was enough.

Next thing on his unwritten list, then, was what he'd been putting off, knowing it had to be done, not exactly dreading it, but wishing in his soul it was unnecessary. Find Fisher Greene.

CHAPTER 36

Turned out to be easier than he'd expected. He'd figured the man to be gone with nobody able to say where. Because Harvey had little doubt it was Greene had tried for him the day before. He drew his revolver and held it beside his leg pointed at the floor as he entered the Frio Saloon.

And there sat Greene at a poker table, reared back on the hind legs of his chair as he examined the cards in his hand. He looked like he had no cares in the world. Harvey walked up behind him, noting the wide-eyed stares of the three others at the table before he reached out with his left hand and jerked the chair over backwards.

The cards flew up like scattering quail. Greene landed hard and Harvey put the gun barrel between the man's eyes. He cocked the hammer and glanced over his shoulder.

"Don't you men try a move on me. I'll blow his head off." They took him at his word and settled back. One of the players, he noticed, was Trey Braca, the freighter Morgan Bailey had mentioned.

"Fisher, I thought you planned to come at me face on."

"I'm not armed, Kitren."

"I heard you was. I heard you had it in mind to shoot me on sight."

Greene made no effort to sit up. "You're thinking it was me ambushed you. I figured as much."

"Get up here. I don't see a gun."

"I told you, I'm not armed."

"That don't mean a thing to me. Pocket gun? I know you slicks like 'em."

Harvey stepped back and Greene sat up. One of the players at the table made a move, not Braca, one of the others. Harvey heard the chair scoot and his boot stabbed backward, catching the man's knee and the hard edge of the chair. The tumble caused a clatter on the wood floor, the pistol butt flying out of a surprised hand.

Two quick steps and Harvey planted the toe of his boot into the fellow's rib cage with a kick that brought a loud yelp. He looked around. "Anybody else want in this?" Didn't seem so. Only two other men there anyhow, plus the bartender, a young fellow Harvey hadn't seen before. The bartender swayed a little, like he might make a move for a hidden weapon. Harvey shook his head. The swaying stopped He glanced down at the would-be gunman. "You stay right still." Pain showed on the man's face from the kick and the sprawl. He tried quick looks from the corners of his eyes, searching the floor for what he'd just lost, not seeing it.

"Come after me again and I'll kill you," Harvey told the bald man. "Lay right there and I'll be out of your way in a second or two."

He caught Fisher Greene's elbow and pulled him up. "Let's go on outside, Fisher."

"I ain't going nowhere with you, Kitren."

"Yes, you are. You walk or I'll knock you in the head and drag you. Make up your mind."

Greene let out a long breath that took his bravado with it. "Hell, let's go."

Harvey followed him outside, paused at the batwing doors and said to the saloon crowd. "We'll be right out here. Be a bad idea if you come out this door before I'm finished. Fair warning."

Greene looked more mad than scared. He turned to face Harvey. "Maybe I give you cause for this, but I was blowing off. I never meant it. And it damned sure was not me in that alley shot you."

Harvey kept his aim on the middle of the man's belly, walked around him so he could look back at the saloon door. The bartender's head poked out. He saw Harvey looking at him and jumped back inside. Two men in range clothes stepped off

100

the walk out into the sandy street and went around them, then back up on the walk, headed toward the cafe down the street. One of them looked back, like he'd noticed Harvey's gun, but went on anyhow.

"You're nothing but a damned bully, Kitren. Ride in here with your ranger's badge, big lawman, demeaning women, shoving that pistol at people minding their own business. Why don't you climb on that pitiful little bay pony and get out of here? Leave people alone?"

Funny thing. Harvey considered the figure in front of him a lowlife, not much better than the snakes that lived along the edge of the river. And yet the words burned. Was there truth in what Greene said? A bully? He hoped not, but this was not the time to think about it.

"Never in my mind to bully anybody, Fisher. I've apologized for what happened, you didn't want it, didn't accept what I had to say, and as far as I'm concerned that is the end of it. But now, somebody, and by that I mean likely you, tried to kill me yesterday."

"I told you. Wasn't me."

"Who, then? One of your buddies in the saloon? Baldy on the floor?"

Greene shook his head. "Them, neither. I don't know who."

Harvey slid the pistol back into its holster and unbuckled his belt. He took the badge out of his pocket and laid the gun rig and the badge on the boards at his feet.

"All right, Fisher. It's not that I believe a word out of your mouth, but it's pointless talking to you. And I got no intention of killing you. So there's my gun and my badge. I'm just plain old Kitren, and I'm saying to your face you're a sorry excuse for a man."

Greene stood staring, as if Harvey spoke some sort of foreign language.

"That's a fair invitation. All that hate of yours, you can turn loose on me. It's a good offer." He waited.

Greene looked down at the gun, then up into Harvey's face. He turned and walked into the saloon without another word.

101

CHAPTER 37

He handed the reins to Ed Caudle. "I just needed to reacquaint us," he said. Believe I'll come early tomorrow and keep him all day.

"I'll be off most of tomorrow, but Manuel works Sundays for me. He'll be here. You get your grave markers up okay?"

"We did. Osgood took care of things in short order."

"I've been thinking about it since you left. None of my business, really, but if you don't object I'll see what I can do to safeguard your effort."

"I don't know what you mean by that."

"Well, I mean I'll stand up in church tomorrow and talk about it. Ask folks to leave the matter be. Is what I meant."

"Sounds like something that would make old Amos mad at you."

"It might, at that. But I've been a friend to the man since he came here. I think he considers me a friend as well. Friendship can stand up to disagreement, I think. If it can't, then it ought to be called something else."

Harvey's route back to the boarding house took him past the saloon. He stepped out into the street as he passed and kept an eye on the door. Nobody showed, but it wouldn't hurt to be careful. He felt grateful for Ed Caudel. The blacksmith seemed to be on his side in all of this. A kind man. He walked down the alley that led past the general store and saw the Forsythe woman drawing water again.

He doffed his hat and said, "Afternoon, ma'am."

She nodded, said nothing in return, and went back to pulling the rope that lifted the well bucket.

"I'll get that for you, if you'll let me."

"Thank you, but no, I'm just fine."

He walked to the back door of the boarding house then turned and watched Pearl Forsythe finish with her chore, pick up her full bucket of water and walk down the alley toward a side door that he supposed opened into the general store.

To Morgan Bailey he said, "That woman gives me kind of a cold shiver."

Morgan glanced up from the pot she was stirring. "Pearl?"

He nodded.

"It's just her way. I been trying to strike up a conversation with her since they came here. Without results."

"Well, it helps to know it's not just me she don't like. Where'd they come from?"

"Moved down from Uvalde a few years back when they took over the store. I think they're from somewhere up in Virginia."

"Who had it before them?" A question that had no particular relevance, but Harvey felt like he hadn't probed near deep enough to learn anything, and he needed a lot more knowledge of this town and its people if he was to have any hope of discovering Ella's killer.

"Oh, same as always. Moneybags Raines. He brought them in to run it. They don't own it."

"Man owns the Double R? And the saloon?"

"And that little bank down the street. Everything else around here it often seems. Gossip is, he struck gold out in California, but who knows?"

He sat on the front porch smoking and watching the day end, now and then a straggling cowboy or sometimes three or four riding up to Lou Campbell's, laughing and nervous. More often drunk and loud. A shame Campbell had to park such as that so close to Morgan Bailey's home and the churchhouse. Looked like there'd be some way to make her move it, but that was just wishful thinking, he figured. Campbell had money, that was plain, and money was what talked loudest.

Rosa came up the front steps and saw him sitting there.

"Evening, Harvey. How you feeling?"

"Pretty good, thanks. I'll be okay in a day or two."

"I prayed for you." She looked a little embarrassed to say it. "I'll be going to church in the morning, if you want to come."

"Believe not, but I thank you for asking." The truth was, he was not sure what he planned to do when morning showed up. Something, though. Something that would get him closer to the answers he'd come for. Time was leaking away.

CHAPTER 38

With no idea why he asked it, he said, "Katy ever go with you?" It was a simple enough question, with no thought behind it, and no insinuation in it, yet it carried something. Must have carried something, because Rosa looked away and shrugged her shoulders. "No. She tried one time, but..." He could guess at the rest.

She said, with a brighter lilt, "See you at supper, then."

All through the meal he felt like an idea was trying to form, but couldn't get a handle on it. It had to do with Katy Wallace, and something somebody had said. Maybe if he just talked to her, talked without all the feelings that seemed to plague them when they were around each other.

Dave Mikeska said, "I heard you was over at the saloon today."

"I was, yeah." He chewed a forkful of beef. He had no intention of discussing it with Mikeska. The man was a gossip and a kind of busybody.

"Fisher and Trey Braca ain't in town if you want to drop over tonight for a drink."

"Not tonight, Dave. Got some things on my mind right now. Where'd they go, those two?"

"Not sure. Out to the Double R, I think. Braca drove his wagon and Fisher rode along. I think Braca's headed on to Eagle Pass and Piedras Negras. He picks up freight there and turns around."

There were two or three different conversations going on at the table, but Katy was as silent as Harvey, paying close attention to her food.

He said, "Katy, when you finish up tonight, I'd like to talk to you if I can."

She looked at him with a wariness, like he might do her harm. "What about?"

And he didn't know how to answer that, because he didn't know, himself. He just wanted to talk, and hoped the talking might lead him to the idea that kept skipping out of reach.

"A couple of things you can help me with."

"Help you?"

He was in no mood for dueling. "How about it?"

"I guess." She didn't sound committed. "Just me and you, you mean? Talking?"

He understood now that she was digging at him. He nodded and went back to his plate. Rosa had turned silent beside him, and his understanding also included the knowledge that he had handed her a small hurt. Nothing he could do about that. She'd taken a liking to him and had built a connection in her own mind that he'd never encouraged.

Morgan spoke up. "You two go on, Katy. I'll get by without you tonight. Go on."

"You sure?"

"Scat, girl."

CHAPTER 39

Katy brought her coffee and held the cup and saucer in her lap while she settled into one of the soft chairs. Harvey had finished his at the table, and felt the lack of anything in his hands. He reached for his tobacco sack and thought better of it. Morgan wouldn't feel kindly for the man who smoked up her parlor.

He felt like he was about to dive into deep water, no matter what he said. And he did not know what he meant to say. Only that he needed to talk to her and listen to her. Since the first time he'd laid eyes on her she had been to him like a streak of color across a gray background, a bloom in the midst of a winter-killed pasture. There was a sort of mystery in that.

"Yes?" She was waiting for him. She lifted her cup off its saucer and brought it to her lips and put it back.

"I'm slow with words, Katy. You and me, we have had no real conversation. Just little snips of talk here and there. So I don't know you, and you don't know me. Not really."

"Well," she said, "I know *of* you. And now you know *of* me. That's a start, I guess."

"You said you were a friend to Ella."

"We're just gonna jump over to the whorehouse, I guess. That what you want to talk about?" She didn't look happy.

"I want to know more of anything you can tell me about her. Not the place—that place. About Ella."

"That's a dark spot in my life. I don't like to think about it. It was a dumb mistake and I'm trying to make it right." She took in a deep breath and expelled it and set the cup and saucer on the floor beside her chair.

She said, "All right. I was only over there three days and two nights, trying to get up my nerve to join in. You

107

understand what I mean by that. I never got to know her then. It was later, after I left, and would run into her walking down by the river sometimes. Just walking, you know, soaking up some sunshine. Lou's women get no welcome anywhere in town. It was just now and then we talked a little."

He thought of the time he'd spent today at the river's edge, staring into the twisting current. Ella had taken her confusion to the same place, looked into the same current. "And that's where you got the idea she was hooked up with some man around here."

"That's right."

"Somebody she loved, I guess you're telling me."

"Yes."

"But you got no idea who."

"No, none at all. She was careful about it. She did seem to be thinking about following after me. Leaving Lou, I mean. But she wanted to stay close here and nobody would have her, after so long..."

"Seems like the town took you in, never mind your past." That sounded like a harsh judgement in his own ears, but she didn't react.

"Yes. Miz Pruett gave me a job at the cafe."

"You could have gone home, couldn't you? Ella could have come with me." He was turning the talk in a way he didn't want to go—into some kind of accusation against Katy. "I don't mean to sound like I'm judging you, Katy. Truly. There's just so much pain around it all, it jumps out when I don't mean for it to."

She let herself smile. "Okay, Harvey. That was good. That was nearly conversation I know you're hurting over Ella. I make allowance for it."

"So when was that? How long ago did you spend that time at Lou's?"

"Last fall. A little over a year ago, I guess."

"And you have not been there any time since?"

The question made her unhappy again. She reached for the coffee cup, leaving the saucer on the floor. She drank from the cup and put it back down, leaning over. "What's your reason for asking that?"

He shrugged. "I don't know. There's something in the back of my mind that I missed, something somebody said or I heard mentioned. Seems like I had the impression you were there the night it happened."

"No." Her voice softened. "I was long gone, and I never went back. I was right here that night, in my room reading a dime novel by lamplight."

He sat there in silence for a long time—five minutes or so. She kept silent, too, finishing her coffee, the big clock in the corner ticking away the time. Harvey tried to put in order the things she'd said, the things he'd learned elsewhere, but nothing stayed in place, nothing raised itself up and said *look at me.*

"I guess I'm keeping you from things," he said. "There's nothing else I can think of to ask."

"You're keeping me from nothing," she said. "I'm a woman alone with a bad past. I live from day to day."

"Where's your home? Why don't you just go back to it?"

She shook her head. "No home anymore. My folks died in a fire years back. Down by San Antonio. Hate to sound pitiful, but I'm alone in the world. And that's how I ended up at Lou's. I found out real quick, though, I am not cut out for that kind of life."

"I'd figure a woman like you—by that I mean a woman as pretty as you, and one that can cook a top-notch blackberry cobbler, would be picked off by a man pretty quick."

"Think again, then. I came to Stampede to work in a whorehouse, and there's nobody here that does not know it. Men included. Think about yourself and how you've behaved toward me since you found out. Well, that's men."

All true, but an unwelcome thing to hear. "You could leave."

"I could. I may. And I'll decide when. And I don't recall asking your advice on the subject." She picked up cup and saucer and got up from the chair. Harvey felt something jump into his throat. He hadn't meant to insult her. Sitting with her, talking, had been a comfort, had been a welcome interlude from loneliness, from the constant chasing, like a dog after its tail, of the days here. He hated for it to end. The clock struck eight.

"I'd Like to show you something."

That got her attention. She'd been like a bird about to spread its wings and fly away, but she paused. "Show me what?"

"It's in my room. Will you look at it?"

"I asked you what. What you're talking about."

"Come on. I'll show you."

CHAPTER 40

She stared at him for what seemed a very long time, then breathed a sigh and followed him into his room. They left the door open. He lit the kerosene lamp beside the bed, went to the saddlebag where it lay on the floor and brought out the knife he'd found. As he brought it out he noticed a smell came with it, just a faint tinge of rusted iron, or blood. When he unwrapped it and showed it to her, Katy stepped back. Her eyes showed shock at the sight.

"I found this the other night. In that shed by the well. You got any idea who put it there?" He watched her face, trying to read what he saw there, feeling all along that it was a surprise to her.

"No. I mean, I don't go in there much. I bring a tub into my room. But no, I never saw that thing. What's on the blade? That's not blood is it?" He believed he saw truth in her expression and heard it in her voice. And that brought a relief to him. Lifted a weight that he hadn't realized he carried. Had he suspected her? Maybe.

"I think it's the knife that killed Ella."

"Wrap it back up. I don't like looking at it."

"I want you to look at it. Tell me if you've ever seen it before. Or one like it."

"Did you check the knives in our kitchen?"

"I showed it to Morgan. She said it's not hers."

"I don't think so. Uh-uh." She shook her head slowly. "It's not new. The blade's been sharpened a lot. Comes from somebody's kitchen, looks like to me."

"Yeah, I think so too." He wrapped it in the bandanna again and put it back in the saddlebag. "Whoever left it hid it well. It was just luck I saw it, jammed inside a crack." He wiped his

111

hands on his pants legs. It seemed like the scent of the knife blade stayed on him.

"You're thinking the person who stabbed your sister left Lou's place on foot, then. Is that right? Then came down the alley behind this house and hid the knife in our shed." She paused and looked into her empty coffee cup like she might find something in it. "I'll bet you're right, Harvey. But I don't know how much help it is if what you want is finding the killer."

"You know it's what I want."

"Why'd you show it to me?"

The question caught him off guard. He understood now why he'd done it, although he'd brought her in here without understanding his own motive. He didn't know what to say.

"You thought it might have been me did it. You wanted to see how I'd react."

"No, yeah, maybe. I don't know, Katy. I'm sorry for the offense. I know you had nothing to do with it."

"You misunderstand me. I don't blame you a bit. It was smart to show me that thing and watch how I'd behave. Now, I'm one less you have to suspect." She seemed sincere, but he was slow to trust the words.

"You've cleared some things up for me, Katy. I thank you."

Long after she'd gone, long after he'd pulled the bedcovers to his chin and closed his eyes, he was still asking himself what it was she'd cleared up.

CHAPTER 41

The sun came up like it was tired, like it had been working hard somewhere under the horizon, and maybe needed more sleep. Sort of the way Harvey was feeling. The bitter coffee off Caudel's forge felt heavy in his stomach, moving inside him with the cadence of the bay pony's gait. He saw the ruts left along the trail by Trey Braca's wagon the day before—ruts caved in by horse tracks here and there, probably Fisher riding alongside or behind the wagon. So they had come out here, just as Dave Mikeska had told him. On their way where? Had to be the Double R, nothing else along here except the Indian's cabin, and it was doubtful they had come for tooth pulling.

Of course, the trail, which could be called a road by a charitable man, which Harvey was not at the moment, went on down toward Eagle Pass and the border. Piedras Negras. Black Rocks. The Mexican town just over the line. He didn't know how far away that was from here, but it had be at least a hard day's ride. Maybe two with a wagon, if that was the destination. Hadn't Morgan Bailey said that the freighter included that trip on his route?

Riding was good. It always was. And the countryside in the early morning felt like a dose of good medicine. This out here was the best part of the state in his opinion. He'd been all over Texas, the pine woods on the east, the big thicket spread out along the gulf, up into the windscoured north and along the low-slung southern coastline with its Spanish missions and its farms. This was best. Hills, clean rivers, limestone and live oaks. Riding through it felt good. For a little while he forgot his little sister had died an ugly death. No, he didn't forget, exactly. He would never forget it. But for just a minute or two he could let it go—just a minute or two—and breathe the clean air and

113

watch fog lift off the new sun and feel his own head clear of last night's fog. Feel his pony's free and rambling spirit invade his own body, let the steady touch of hooves on dirt blow him along this trail like a wayward leaf.

They reached the creek that led up to McDonald's cabin. The pony wanted a drink. Harvey got out of the saddle and rolled a smoke. The horse drank the cold water and then began cropping the tender grasses growing along the bank.

He inhaled the sweet smoke, watching the coal burn down, undecided. Not a good thing when you wore a Ranger badge. You had to pay attention. You had to know where you were and why. Or you needed to give back the badge and find something else to work at. And here he'd come off with not even a hunch or a hint as to the purpose of his ride. It had just seemed when he woke up after the long night that an answer was out here if it was anywhere.

Take Deke McDonald for instance. Eighty acres. What could you do with eighty acres? Not make a living, that was for sure. Especially in droughty times like these. You could run three or four cows on it right now, and that's all. But there the man was, pulling teeth and hoeing a garden. And he was friends with that talkative artist fellow that painted pictures of the range and sketched the faces of women. Didn't make much sense. Didn't fit.

Alright, then. Nobody owed him any answers, but it was time to ask questions. The cabin wasn't far.

CHAPTER 42

The dog began barking as Harvey tied the reins in the same spot he'd used before. The dog was nowhere to be seen, though. The barks, deep and powerful and unhappy, came from behind the little shed that sat near McDonald's cabin. He remembered the size of that animal, a dog big and strong enough to take down anybody. The cabin door stood open. Harvey kept his hand on the pistol butt as he edged around the side of the building. The dog saw him and began another round of noise. The white beast lay on his side and only his head moved. His hindquarters were coated with dried blood. The barking trailed off and stopped. The big head dropped back to the ground.

"Hey there, feller," Harvey said. He knelt beside the heaving chest. The blood was dried dark and solid. And what had bled out onto the ground had formed a pool and then soaked into the ground, leaving just an outline of its shape. The dog's curly white hair was matted and caked with it.

"I see you been out here a while." All night, it looked like. He kept his voice low and slow. Talking seemed to calm the dark eyes. The frantic breathing slowed. He chanced a hand on the thick coat at the dog's shoulder. He felt trembling muscles and smelled the stink of blood. Gunshot wound. Somewhere in the hindquarters, maybe close to the backbone. Harvey stood. "Bring you some water in a minute, friend. Hold on."

First, though, that open door had to be walked through. McDonald didn't do this to his own dog. He dreaded going in the cabin. Hoped he wouldn't find that man dead on the floor. Somebody had done some shooting here last night.

He went through it fast, crouched, his pistol steadied across his left arm, the way he liked to do it. Nobody was inside, dead or alive.

Harvey slid the gun back in its holster and looked around. One of the chairs lay broken on the floor, the little table was moved out of place. Nothing else. It all looked the same as it had on his first visit. It was not the same, though. Somebody had come here and done harm.

The dog was able to cock his head and lap water from the shallow dish Harvey put down. He knelt again. A sharp rock bit into his knee and he shifted to a softer spot. The muscles still trembled under his careful touch, but not as bad as before. "What am I gonna do about you, mister? I need to get on after your boss man, see what's happened to him, and here you lay dying or maybe paralyzed and can't do things for yourself."

Wouldn't it be best? Wouldn't it be the decent thing to do...a quick shot behind this poor fellow's ear?

"Maybe would," he answered his own silent thought. "Maybe would. But not now. You may come to yourself yet. Could be you just need a little time. And I'm the man can give it to you. You rest. I'm about to look for something we can eat."

He had it in mind to scramble some eggs and share them with the wounded pup, but found none inside the cabin. He did find a half-dozen biscuits in the safe, though they were probably left over from a meal yesterday or last night and had turned hard. Didn't matter. No nests inside the coop, just roosting perches. He remembered seeing chickens scratching around in the garden and sure enough there were three nests on the back wall of the shed right where the dog lay. Harvey hadn't thought to look inside them. The nests were made of bushel baskets and filled with straw, their bottoms nailed to the planks of the shed.

One was empty, but he found three brown eggs in the second, and then two white ones in the third. Not as many as he'd like, but it would do.

He was impatient with the kindling, got a fire going and located some lard. When he carried half—maybe a little less than half—of the cooked eggs outside there stood the white dog next to the porch. Harvey set the plate down where McDonald's pet could reach it. "Careful. It's still hot," he said. "I'm glad to see you on your feet."

The food was gone before he went back inside. He ate the rest of it fast, worrying about what he ought to do with the dog. Closest neighbor would be the Double R headquarters, but that felt like a bad idea. Have to leave him here. Nothing to do about it. No other choice. He stuck one of the biscuits in his pocket and left the rest on the floor.

The dog must have weighed a hundred pounds. Getting him up the steps and inside the cabin was a struggle. Harvey set a bucket of water beside the biscuits and pulled the quilt off the narrow bed. He folded it twice and made a pallet. "You lay yourself down right there. You got a little to eat, and you got some water. I'll shut this door now and you can rest. I'll be back quick as I can."

CHAPTER 43

The pony had wandered along the edge of the trees surrounding McDonald's cabin, reins trailing on the ground, searching out the browning clumps of grass among the clutter of fallen leaves. Acorns crunched under Harvey's boots as he walked. The tannic odor of acorns and fallen leaves was in the air, This year's crop was small because of the drought, but that flowing creek must be spring-fed. It kept a narrow strip of country damp and green. Must be why McDonald had built his cabin here.

In the saddle, Harvey felt his lack of decision again. Where to? His mount was anxious, pulling at the bit. "Whoa, now. Set still a second" he left the reins slack, took out the biscuit and ate it sitting there. Might be all the food he got today. The biscuit finished, wishing for a cup of coffee, he aimed west along the creek toward the trail that led to the Raines ranch.

On the lane coming up from the house a team of six horses pulled an open wagon. The six were a mixed bunch of the work breeds, with hooves big as dinner plates. Perched on a bench up in the front sat Trey Braca with his hat low over his eyes. Smoke circled his face. A black cigar was parked in his mouth. Harvey stopped and waited for the man to come abreast. He smelled the raw stink of cigar smoke and wondered again what caused people to smoke the things. For a second it looked like Braca was going to ignore him and drive on past, but then the freighter lifted his long reins and pulled back on the lead horse. The lead was the only one with a bit in his mouth and reins to guide him. The others followed the lead. The wagon halted. Braca took off his hat with one hand and with the other

118

removed his cigar, then spit tobacco juice onto the ground next to Harvey. His face carried no expression. "Howdy."

These wagons most often didn't have seats of any kind for the driver. Instead, most drivers rode on the Lazy Board that jutted out from the left side. Many times they didn't ride at all, but walked alongside, leaving more room for freight and less weight for the team to pull..

The wagon bed was empty.

"My name's Kitren."

"The ranger."

"That's right." The man didn't offer his own name.

"And you're Trey Braca. I understand you run freight through here."

"That's my job." He put the cigar back in his mouth and replaced his hat. "I work for Roy Raines back there." He gestured over his shoulder.

"I rode out to talk to Raines. He at home?"

"Oh, yeah. I just talked to him."

"Fisher down there, too?"

"He'll catch up to me in a little while."

"I guess you're headed back to Stampede."

"What business is it of yours where I'm headed? Still a free country, ain't it?"

"Mostly it is, yeah."

"I know you push folks around, Ranger, but don't try it on me. I push back, if you know what I mean."

Braca puffed hard on the cigar, made the end of it glow red, slapped the reins against his lead's rump and yelled "Heyahhh!" The wagon lurched ahead. Harvey sat still and let it move on. Had they hauled an empty wagon out here? Didn't seem likely.

The bay pony started to follow after the wagon. Harvey wheeled him around and said, "Sorry, friend. We got some business down the road."

119

CHAPTER 44

They'd seen him coming. Three men stood on the porch watching as he rode up. He waited for an invitation to dismount, didn't get it, and stepped off the pony anyhow. The three waited in the shade of the porch, all hatless, Fisher Greene's bald scalp as shiny white as a cue ball in a billiards parlor. The cook who'd fed Harvey on his last trip out here fidgited beside Greene, ill at ease over something they'd been discussing.

The third man had to be Roy Raines, owner of this ranch and from what Harvey had been told, a big chunk of everything else from here to Stampede, and most of Stampede as well. There was an air about him. You couldn't miss it. He was in his forties, about Harvey's age, maybe a little older. He was tall and slender, graceful looking as he stepped off the porch to shake Harvey's hand.

Well, dressed, too, in range clothes that had never seen a day of hard work. The hand smooth and uncallused. The thick hair long and blond and the smile open and sincere. Braca back there had smelled like cigar smoke. This fellow smelled like money.

"I'm Roy Raines, Mister Kitren." The accent was southern, not Texan. Made Harvey think of the soldier boys he'd known from the Carolinas, Virginia and the like.

"You ain't welcome here, Kitren," Greene said, walking out of the porch shadow. He was armed with a holstered pistol.

"Now Fisher, this man is a law officer," Raines said in that same soft drawl. He kept the friendly smile on his face. The rancher wore no gun. Harvey didn't trust the smile or the handshake. This was a nest of wasps.

He turned his attention back to Harvey and said, "You know Fisher, of course, and Dixie, who keeps us well-fed. As a matter of fact, I understand he fed you a few days ago. Which answers the question of how I already knew your name. How can I help you?"

Harvey decided this one was as long-winded as Cee Tims. The cook spoke up. "Mister Raines, I better go get something on the stove. Hands'll show up hungry before long."

"Sure, Dixie. You go ahead." He turned back to Harvey and waited.

"I was hoping to talk to one of your wranglers again. Fellow by the name of Welty."

Raines nodded his head and the wide smile turned serious. "Luther Welty. You talked to him last time."

"It's why I showed up out here. Tracked him to Deke McDonald's place. Getting a tooth pulled."

"Just out of curiosity, why'd you want to talk to Luther?"

"I'd rather keep that to myself." Harvey was already tired of this strained conversation. "Where can I find him?"

"Abilene, far as I know."

"Gone from here?" It was not surprising. Ranch hands moved around from place to place. Especially this time of year when work slowed down and the cow crowd thinned out. "He coming back?"

"Not likely. Drew his pay and moved on. I said Abilene because his folks live up that way is what he told me. But you know, I can't be sure of it." A sudden gust of wind brought the smell of wood smoke. Harvey saw a cloud of it rise out of the cook shack chimney. That'd be Dixie the cook stoking a fire.

He said, "Well, much obliged. I guess I rode out for nothing." He caught the reins in his left hand and swung into the saddle. "Think I'll stop off at McDonald's place, see how he's gettin' along. You seen him lately?"

Fisher Greene stayed ramrod straight, staring hard. Raines's smile didn't falter. He said, "No, Deke hasn't visited us in a while. Say hello if you see him."

At the top of the lane Harvey eased the reins onto the bay's neck and turned him north, feeling the tiny thrum of excitement through the horse's ribs. It caused him to smile at nothing in particular. "Thinking about oats, I guess. I'm a mind reader when it comes to you." A quarter mile ahead, just short of a bend in the trail, sat Braca's wagon. The team stood unmoving except for their tails fanning at flies of one kind or another. Braca himself was on the ground, bent over the right front wheel. As Harvey rode closer the man stood up and seemed to notice him for the first time.

Harvey called out. "Trouble?" A rifle cracked twice, one behind the other. The horse was hit. He felt the bay lose his footing, try to rear and then fall, spinning onto his left side, Harvey's leg pinned against the rocky ground. He grabbed for his pistol, got hold of it, then the hurt pony screamed and tried lunging back on his feet. The sudden movement caused Harvey to drop his weapon, holding to the saddle horn, hoping the little pony could carry them out of this mess, a mess he should have expected, should have watched out for. From somewhere in the brush beside the road the rifle fired again.

A boulder dropped off a high place might feel like that, he thought, might halt your breath, crush your will and your hope and press you down into the dirt. And then he stopped thinking of anything at all and let go of himself.

CHAPTER 45

Ella's voice. *Am I dead? Ella?* His mouth tasted metallic, like a penny floating in his spit, or a fired .45 shell. Or blood. Yes, blood. *They shot. Me. My pony? Killed my pony.* He forced the grief of it from his thoughts. Not now. Breathing was hard. The air seemed thick and heavy. The voice again. A woman? Not Ella. Ella was dead. But a woman. Somewhere distant. The woman laughed. Men laughed. The talk sounded hollow, in a barrel, echoing. Her voice was pitched high like a bell, the men darker, a curse or a threat.

A man groaned close by. Harvey tried opening his eyes and couldn't. Wait. He thought to use a hand to force them open. It didn't work. He tried locating his arms and hands and after a while knew they were tied behind him, lashed together by something. A rope? And the weight of his body lay on his arms.

He tried again to open his eyes, both crusted and stuck together. He rolled his head to the right and tried rubbing his cheek on his shoulder. An eyelid worked itself free and lifted. But there was nothing to see. He was surrounded by pitch black. Was it nighttime? Could he have been out that long?

He could still hear voices coming from somewhere near, one woman and two or three men. He thought he recognized Fisher Greene's croak, a safe guess but hard to be sure.

They'd played him like a fool and he'd acted the part, all right. A lawman all these years, all the dangers he'd fought his way past, and here he lay trussed and maybe dying in the dark. Rode right up and invited a potshot. Somebody complied. Poor little pony. And poor ranger, too, looked like. His chest hurt with every breath of the heavy air. The nearby man groaned again.

"Who are you?" He whispered. The effort to speak caused more pain. His mouth felt swollen and stiff, his teeth too big. He waited, but heard no response. He tried again, gritting his big teeth against the hurt. A flutter of movement then, felt as much as heard, as if the deep darkness were solid and movement rippled through it like ripples in water.

"...You?" It was not so much a word as it was a sigh and a groan, a cloud drifting past. But it was enough. He knew the voice.

"Deke. It's Kitren. You understand me?" He waited, ignoring the pain slicing through his chest like a dull knife.

"Harvey?" Clearer this time, louder, the man coming up from somewhere else.

"Keep it down. Just whisper. There's people close by."

"What're you doing here?"

"I don't know. Somebody shot me. Next thing I'm laying here."

"Raines. Greene. That bunch."

"Yeah, I figured. You hurt bad?"

"Hard to say. I guess so. Concussion, I think. Greene knocked me in the head with his pistol. You?"

"Seem to be. Got a hole in my chest. Hurts to breathe."

McDonald didn't say anything else for long seconds, then, "I don't hear a sucking sound. Maybe it didn't get you in the lung." The echoing voices grew fainter and vanished, as if the speakers had gone.

Harvey said, "What is this, anyhow? Where are we?"

"Cave." An answer Harvey had not expected, but sure—the echo, the darkness, the sense of desolation pressing down.

"Are we still on the Double R?"

"Oh, yes. Raines' silver mine."

"I didn't know there was silver in this part of the country."

"There's not."

CHAPTER 46

Harvey knew that silver had been harvested in Texas in the early days. Legend was, the Spaniards had mined it up on the San Saba long time back. Melted it down into ingots shaped like lizards. Iguanas. Then shipped most of it back to Spain, before they got themselves massacred by Indians. Story was, Jim Bowie found the place it was stored, but then got massacred himself at the Alamo before he could do anything about it. It was called *Las Iguanas* or *the Lost Jim Bowie Mine.* And the stories were true. Harvey knew they were. Not long ago he'd held one of those silver iguanas in his hand and had thrown it into a creek near the Pedernales river crossing. The things had caused too much death and destruction and he carried no personal appetite for wealth as some men did. He had thought no more about that time, until now.

Men's voices had returned to the cave and were moving in their direction, growing louder.

Shadows mixed with a flickering light that played along uneven walls, showing Harvey for the first time the boundaries of the place that held him. Stacks of something, boxes, piled high just a couple of yards away, then Fisher Greene's smile behind the coal-oil lantern he was holding. The small flame of it seemed bright as the sun after the total midnight of the cave. Trey Braca walked abreast of Greene around the wide bend. Just those two, nobody else. Harvey wondered who the woman had been, and where she'd gone.

Braca said, "I see you're still alive, Ranger, but don't get used to it. Things is about to change."

"I waited til you woke up, Kitren. Wouldn't been no fun if you couldn't feel it," Fisher Greene said. He handed the lantern over to Braca and stepped up closer. A smudge of smoke came off the lantern, and the stink of burning kerosene. He swung his right leg back and kicked hard. The sharp-toed boot bit into Harvey's ribs near the bullet wound. Then a second time.

Harvey heard a protest from McDonald, then felt a third kick and the pain was so great it ran across him like a lightning strike. Things turned red and he fell over into quiet unknowing again.

The wakeup was quick and painful. He felt himself lifted, shoulders and feet, and dumped onto what felt like a wood floor. Horses snorted. He was in Braca's wagon. The sun skipped across his face, high overhead and bright. Still not far past noontime. These things were all happening fast. Deke lay next to him. The man's head was bloody. Much of it had run down his face and dried into the shirt he wore. Harvey's chest and shoulders hurt worse than before. Greene's boots had seen to that. He considered that maybe it was deserved, since he himself had meted out a similar punishment a long time back at the foot of the whorehouse stairs. The boxes he'd first seen in the cave were long wooden crates, stacked around him, leaving just enough room for the two men. A canvas sheet now slid over it all, Braca snugging it down, covering the wagon cargo, shutting out the sun. In the narrow space he smelled steel and something else—raw and meaty. Tallow?

Raines' voice then. "Don't worry about it, Fisher. Just to be safe, take both of them across the border. Do whatever you want then, but neither one of them comes back. Understand?"

"Yeah, I understand."

"And nothing rough between here and there. You had your fun."

"We won't get there tonight. Have to make camp."

"I know that, but I want you gone. I want them out of here before somebody comes looking. If either one dies along the way take the body on with you. And I'll tell you again—don't kill 'em this side of the border. Leave it for the Mexicans to worry with."

Silence after that, the sound of a single horse fading into the distance, then the rattle of harness and stamping hooves. Curses from Braca, short barks of laughter from Fisher Greene. Harvey felt the wagon bounce on its springs as somebody—

Braca, he supposed—climbed to the bench seat. Reins slapped,
Braca yelled "eyup!" and they were moving.

CHAPTER 47

Tree limbs slapped at the sides of the wagon and scraped their way across the canvas covering. Rocks rolled under the hooves of the animals pulling them. The overhead sun smeared a muted light into the stingy pocket of space around Harvey and Deke.

Deke said, "They're gonna take us across the border and kill us."

Harvey whispered back, "Yeah. I heard."

"I thought Greene already killed you. Back there in the cave," Deke said.

"Feels like he did." The wagon was on springs, but the springs didn't do much in the way of cushioning the ride. Jolt after jolt shook Harvey as the wheels stumbled their way over rocks and fallen limbs.

"Your dog's alive."

"What?"

"Yeah, hurt bad, but I fed and watered him and put him in your cabin."

"They shot him first thing, Fisher did." The Indian's whisper was so thin Harvey could barely make out the words. "I would've sworn he was finished. Well...thanks. Maybe he'll survive, even if we don't."

"I hate to admit that I don't much understand what's going on." Harvey turned away from the other man, onto his left side, easing the burden on his arms and hands still tied behind his back. It helped a little, but made breathing harder and added to the feeling of broken glass inside his torso. "How'd they get you in their sights, anyhow?"

"Raines had his suspicions. He was watching and waiting. I knew they were setting up for another run to the border, and figured I'd wait for night and come for a look see. They came for me first. Showed up out of nowhere. Rat in a trap."

Deke managed to inch himself closer. "It's a long story. I ain't got the strength to tell it, either. They worked me over some more when they finished with you."

"What's these crates? You know?"

"Guns."

"I don't know of a law says they can't haul guns if they want to."

"Another revolution building over there. Raines is supplying guns. He buys them, steals them, whatever, stores them in that cave, then makes a run to Piedras Negras."

"But still, I mean, why all that trouble?"

"The Mexican government. They don't want the rebels building up for it. Federales will confiscate the arms if they find them."

That made a little sense, Harvey thought. Maybe. But it was a long way from explaining why Raines and these other two were willing to do murder. In his own case it could just be the spite of Fisher Greene. But in Deke's case there had to be more to it—much more.

"What about silver? The silver mine?" This whispering business was beginning to feel like work, but it helped, because otherwise there was nothing but motion and stagnant heat and the worry of what lay ahead.

He waited for an answer, but got none. He turned his head enough so that he could see Deke's bloody shirt and head. The man's eyes were closed.

"Deke?"

"Yeah, sorry. I went spinning off for a little bit there. Cold sweat."

"Well, just be quiet if you need to. I'll stop pestering."

"I'm okay now. The silver. He buys it from Mexican mines. Claims he digs it on his ranch."

"No law against that, either."

"Mexican law. He buys it cheap, the mines don't pay taxes, Mexico wants the taxes."

Okay, now he began to understand what was happening. Some of it, anyhow. He fought off the pain and nausea that

129

threatened to push him back into the dark, quiet place. He whispered, "What about you? How come you're in this?"

The answer came back quick, like it was waiting on Deke's lips, the man knowing the question was coming. "Pinkerton."

"You mean that detective bunch up north?"

"Yeah. Mexicans hired us, sent me down here to watch."

And with that everything slid into place and Harvey understood at last the outline of the goings on that had caught him up and was pretty soon now going to eat him up.

CHAPTER 48

The sudden stop of the wagon yanked him awake. He'd been asleep despite the aches and a sense of doom, feelings that stayed with him. Footsteps on leaves, the snorting of the work team. Little light squeezed through the canvas now. Must be near sundown. Hours had passed, then, while they rolled toward the border. He turned his head, ignoring the crease of pain that traveled down his neck into his spine.

Two open eyes stared at him.

"Deke?"

No movement and no response. He smelled smoke. They'd built a campfire.

He called out, "Fisher, you need to see about McDonald."

"Shut up Ranger. I don't need to do nothing."

"I think he's dead."

The canvas lifted. More smoke rolled in, a glimpse of an early star just above the treeline. Fisher Greene peered in then reached for the Indian's head and moved it back and forth a couple of times.

"I'm damned if he ain't!"

Harvey felt a sadness make its way through the hurt and the helplessness. Not grief, exactly; he'd barely known the man, but known him enough to believe him upright and honest and his loss a loss to whatever was decent in a difficult world.

"How long he been dead?"

"I don't know." Harvey had trouble pushing the words out. His body had gone weak and shaky, and he wondered how much was left of time, energy, even the will to fight. "I was asleep."

Greene dropped the canvas and Harvey heard the man's footsteps through dry leaves. From a distance he heard, "McDonald's kicked the bucket, Trey."

131

Then the freighter. "Well, we stomped him pretty good back there. Probably got to bleeding in his head."

Greene said, "The thing is, do we leave him here or carry him on with us?"

"I ain't no mind reader, but I'd wager Raines would say take him on, drop him somewhere over the line."

"Seems spooky to me, traveling with a dead man."

"Won't be but half a day or so. We can stand it." The two of them laughed.

He would drop off to sleep, then come awake like he'd been slapped, the vision of McDonald's eyes etched in the dark space around him. It went on like that all night.

The detail and color of the gaze rolled around inside Harvey's head, half-dream, half-thought, and after a while he began to believe that he was losing his mind. The eyes were brown, and they slanted a little with the Indian blood. The whites grew wider and wider, like when a horse is scared and shows it. White as a lantern flame and staring at him unblinking.

Greene and Braca had offered him no food or water, and he had not cared. They'd get no satisfaction if they expected him to beg. Water would have been a mercy, but he'd done without it many times in the past. Food, too. Through the canvas he'd smelled their coffee and fried meat and their tobacco smoke; listened to the drone of their voices and their snores, tried to think of a way out of this, but could not. After a very long time the night crawled to the edge of things and slid away.

CHAPTER 49

"Open your mouth." Greene used one hand to turn Harvey's head, the other to pour water from a jug. The water washed over his face, into his nose and hair. Into his eyes. He managed to do as the big man told him, and felt his mouth fill up with it, couldn't swallow fast enough, and then as he understood what was happening, the pour stopped.

He heard Trey Braca call out, "Don't waste our water, Fisher."

"Why, hell, man, Raines wants him alive to the border. Just a drink, that's all. He ain't had none for a day now." The canvas fell back and he was in the dark again. He could still taste the water. He'd gotten just enough down to make him want more. On the other hand, even that brief couple of swallows might help him stay alert, stay alive. The space around him held a new smell, like meat turning bad.

He listened to the sounds of the two men moving around, getting the wagon set to travel. Low talking, snorts of laughter, grunts, the rattle of harness and the throaty protests of the work team as they were hitched up, their hooves rattling on the rocky ground. Harvey pictured it all in his head, feeling trapped and at the mercy of cruel men and fate. His belly cramped and he thought for a second he might throw up the little bit of water. He held his breath and waited and it settled down again, leaving him with a sense of weakness and futility.

Had he ever been so helpless? Not that he could remember, and there'd been some rough times, all right. Worst part was, he'd let it happen. There was plenty of warning if a man paid attention. The wounded dog, McDonald missing. Somehow, he'd overlooked the danger, underestimated these men, and now they had him. Helpless. Regret sharp as slivered flint cut

133

through him, rage at himself and the two smug kidnappers. He fought against the ropes that bound him, rolled forward and back, gritting his teeth, twisting his arms until he felt skin and muscle giving way, as though it might tear loose from his bones. He had no more strength, no more hope. Time passed and his breathing slowed little by little. He cut off thinking and let the feelings blow through him like a windstorm. After a time he dozed again.

The lack of movement woke him. He listened. How long had he been asleep? There was no conversation, no footsteps, no indication Greene or Braca were anywhere close. Then there came the familiar sound of hooves on rock, the scratch of brush across saddle leather. A horse trotting closer and halting, Fisher Greene's voice.

"Duncan's occupied again."

"What? Ain't been no soldiers there for years."

"Well, go look for yourself, you don't believe me. There's a couple dozen horses pastured, and the stars and stripes waving from the flagpole."

"I wonder how come I ain't heard nothing about it? Looks like Raines would've found out, don't it?"

"I don't know. What I do know is, we got to find another crossing. Them bluebellies catch sight of us they going to want to see what we hauling."

"What if they got patrols out?"

"Could be, I guess."

Braca said, "I don't need to be carrying no dead man if they come across us. No ranger, neither."

"But you're okay about contraband guns, huh?" Greene laughed. "If you're scared, maybe we better just turn around and go home."

"No, Mister Raines is an unmerciful man. He'd expect us to think ourselves through the problem. The Mexicans is probably over there now waiting for the guns."

CHAPTER 50

Silence again. He heard Greene get down from his horse. The scent of cigar smoke drifted through the canvas over Harvey's head. A nasty stench like always, but it covered the bad-meat smell. So the army had occupied Fort Duncan again. It was one of several forts along the Rio Grande unused and vacant since the beginning of the war. The river ferry downhill from the fort gave easy access to border crossers from both directions. And so that's where they'd been hauling him. Him and the dead Deke McDonald.

The soldiers were likely posted there to stop or impede this very thing—guns smuggled to rebel outfits stirring up another revolution. Benito Juarez had been president a long time. More than one army officer or politician would be ready and willing to take the man's place at the head of the country. By election, by force, or by luck. It didn't seem to matter in Mexico. Power was power, however you could get it. Pretty much like everywhere else, in Harvey's opinion.

The wagon lurched, Braca climbing down. He said, "We ought to bury McDonald. He's stinking and I'm tired of the smell. We need to stay in the brush til dark and find a way across, and that's too long to put up with it."

"Mighty scant brush," Harvey heard Fisher Greene say. Harvey's face felt suddenly flush, hot, hotter than the day, and a shiver ran through him. Fever coming on? It seemed likely, from the beating he'd taken the day before. The kind of beating that had killed the man lying beside him. Every breath was painful. Maybe it would be better all around if they decided to end it right here. A quick bullet and the hurt would be done.

But it wouldn't be a bullet. Not with the Yankee army close by. Something worse. A knife, a rope around his throat, a club against his head. That kind of thing.

Greene went on, "If it's up to me, and I believe it is, we'll leave him be for now. I ain't in the mood to dig and it seems like a needless chance, leaving a body to be maybe found and traced back."

Braca answered, "Suit yourself. I'll walk off a ways from this smell and take me a nap under them mesquites."

"Watch out for thorns. Everything that grows out here seems like is prickly."

They'd left the team hitched to the wagon. Harvey could hear them stomp their feet, and now and then the metallic ring of chains and harness. The smell of Greene's cigar stayed strong, so he hadn't gone far, whatever he was up to. Then the crunch of boots close by.

The canvas flew back. A patch of blue sky winked overhead, a welcome sight. Fisher Green's face blocked it out. The big man took off his hat and ran a hand over his bare scalp.

"Better give you another drink, I reckon." He poised the jug over Harvey's face and began to tip it.

"Don't pour so fast this time." The words came out so weak and thin Harvey didn't at first think the man had heard.

"Well, talk about your beggars and your choosers. Open your mouth." This time it fell into Harvey's mouth slowly enough that he could swallow most of it. He thought nothing had ever tasted so good. He wished it would keep on, but it stopped and left him still thirsty, still needing more. Greene plugged the jug and leaned into the wagon, chewing on his half-burned cigar.

"My partner yonder thinks we ought to send you off to the happy huntin' ground and dig a hole for you and McDonald here."

His voice held amusement in check, but the hateful mouth smiled. Harvey had nothing to say.

"See, what I want is to get halfway across the river and chunk you both in the water. McDonald won't mind, but you,

136

ranger-man, you will drown in dirty water while you float out to the Gulf." He backed off and pulled the canvas part-way closed. He said, "I wanted you to have something you could be thinking about. You can swallow all the water you want then." He laughed, the canvas flopped back into place and Harvey lay in shadow again with his dead friend and his hopeless thoughts.

CHAPTER 51

The rest of the day seemed to last for eternity, nothing but the slow squeeze of time, the burn of fever and the shivers of his wounded body for company. Maybe that's how it would end for him. Not the river, nor a knife or bullet, but maybe the simple inhale of a breath and then no exhale, and all of this pain and sorrow at an end. He almost wished for it. But after that, who was left to speak for Ella? Who would see to it that justice was served for his baby sister? Or himself, for that matter. He would always be the man who rode out one day and never came back. Those thoughts woke him up. They drove out his sense of despair. And bit by bit, into that empty space began to flow back the memory of who he was. What he was. Somewhere beyond the fever and the chills and even the despair, a thought resolved itself. The thought was this—he would survive.

Braca came walking out of the brush. Harvey could hear his careless boots stomp their way over sticks and thorns and thin gravel. "These horses need water. Them tin soldiers are likely at supper by now. Why don't we look for another ford? Bound to be some place we can cross."

The two talked it over in low voices that Harvey didn't try to follow, and then he heard one of them, probably Greene, mount up and ride away. The canvas cover lifted away. Not dark yet, but the sun was down. A cool breeze dipped into the stagnant space and caused him to shiver.

"Open your mouth." It was Trey Braca. "I said open it." The man turned Harvey's head with one hand and stuffed some sort of dirty cloth into Harvey's mouth with the other. Then he pulled a faded red bandanna out of a hip pocket and circled

Harvey's head with it, forcing the wadded cloth deeper into his throat. Braca tied off the contraption with a hard knot and let the ranger's head drop back to the wagon boards. The taste and smell of it caused him to gag. He thought for a second he might throw up and choke, but he managed to swallow, kept it down and tried to work the obstruction up toward his teeth and out of his throat. That helped, but not much.

Breathing was even harder now. It felt like he couldn't get enough air. His face felt swollen and hot and his breathing was a thin, desperate whistle. This was something new. Something he'd never encountered before. This scared him.

"I don't think we'll run into any soldier boys, but in case we do I want you quiet. I hear any commotion out of you I'm liable to just forget what Mister Raines wants. You comprende?"

Harvey offered no answer to the question. Paid it no attention at all. He was too busy fighting for his next breath.

He thought they must have been traveling through woods rather than open country because the scrape of limbs across the canvas cover never stopped. Nor did Braca's curses at his work team. The nasty-tasting thing that filled his mouth was soaked with spit that ran down his throat. His jaw felt tired, forced open like it was. A new ache spread into his ears and face and up the sides of his head. He kept his mind on Ella and vowed a silent vow of revenge. Maybe he'd never be able to keep it, but it helped fight off panic.

Not even sleep could offer escape. It seemed to him he'd surely suffocate if he dozed, so he fought it, and fought the panic and the despair. The wagon stopped. The springs squeaked. Braca jumped to the ground. The thud of his boots seemed loud. Harvey heard a mockingbird sing. He had forgotten about birds during this captive ride that had lasted so very long. The song sounded fine, like water tasted.

Voices? Horses. More than one. He heard Fisher Greene talking to Braca but couldn't make out the words. The teamster climbed back on and popped his reins and the wagon lurched ahead.

After another long time of grinding wheels he heard Greene again. "Just take it slow, now. He says it's axle deep. That a problem for you?"

Braca answered from his perch, "No. This where you want to chunk our passengers?"

CHAPTER 52

This was the river. The Rio Grande or Rio Bravo, depending which side you stood on. The spot where his life was about to end. He caught a brief memory, like a gust of wind, of the colored woman back at Lou's. He owed her a dollar, and felt sorry he'd never be able to pay her. He'd heard drowning was a peaceful way to go, and hoped that was true, but had never asked how anybody knew it for fact.

The wheels were in the current. Water felt its way through the spokes and the steel rims rang on a rocky bed. The smugglers had found a ford and there'd be no help from Fort Duncan, a useless hope he'd discarded anyhow. Braca called out to his team and the wagon stopped. The river sounds kept on.

Soon now the canvas would be thrown back and he'd be in that water, tied and helpless, not even able to yell for help. Someone else was talking to Braca. The voice of a stranger. Higher up, sitting on horseback. Mexican accent. The wagon bounced. Braca was climbing over the guns, coming back for him. A bootheel pressed into Harvey's belly, with the man's weight on it. The pain nearly caused him to black out. The heel moved off him and planted itself on the board bottom beside him. The cover flew back and he was looking up at Braca's face, almost hidden by his stained felt hat. Shadowed by the lowering sun. Braca came down on one knee with a knife in his hand. He reached behind McDonald's body and sliced through the rope they'd bound him with. He had trouble with the arms. They had stiffened as dead arms will and had not yet finished with that stage of death..

The stranger rode closer to the wagon and leaned over. "I'll help you. He caught hold of the arms and said, "Lift now." And the two of them raised the body enough to slide it into the river.

"I won't be missing that smell," Braca said.

The long knife was no more than a couple of inches away from Harvey's face. Braca looked at him, but made no move except the half-smile that curled his lips. "Anybody finds him now, won't be no rope on him. Pore boy fell in and drowned, is all." He left the canvas open and climbed back to his seat. The team of horses responded to Braca's yell and began to pull again. Among all the hurts he felt just then, Harvey managed a few thoughts of prayer for the man now tumbling in the Rio Grande current. Not much of a funeral service, but all that could be had.

In half a minute the river sounds were behind them and Harvey was still alive. He smelled water and mud and the plants that grew along the riverbank, and the leftover stink of Deke McDonald. The wagon tilted up an incline, but the rough boards kept him in place. He wished to hear another mockingbird sing, but there was only the sound of horse hooves and turning wheels.

More of the same while he wondered why they hadn't thrown him out too, as Fisher Greene had threatened. It was small consolation. Worse treatment was to come.

Then he saw the thick growth of live oaks overhead. Heard the voices of men, some speaking Spanish. Smelled smoke from a campfire. This was the spot they'd been heading for all these hours. The rendevous point. The spot where they would trade the guns for silver and head back. Head back without Harvey.

The back gate lifted off and Harvey tried to see into the distance, get some idea of where the river lay, but the low sweep of oak limbs blocked his view. Then two pairs of rough hands reached for him and pulled him to the ground. There stood Braca again with his knife.

142

CHAPTER 53

"Didn't mean to scare you Ranger." He smiled his half-smile and cut the ropes away from Harvey's arms. There was no feeling at all in his hands and fingers after two days of this treatment. He brought his arms out to the side and tried rubbing his hands over the ground. Maybe that would help get the blood flowing again into the near-ruined flesh. Somebody else, a man in a sombrero, untied the bandanna and Harvey at last spit out the foul wad that had plagued him. He could breathe again. That was enough for right now. A bad time was coming, but he could breathe again.

As best he could tell there were three strangers camped here. The one who'd come to meet the wagon and two others. They also had a wagon parked under the trees. A small one, less than half the size of Braca's. Easy to see they were Mexicans. Dressed in rough garb with the big hats on their heads.

A shadow crossed his face and two boots stepped close. One of them drew back and kicked him in the head, on the very spot of the wound from days before. He felt the stitches tear loose from the blow, and a pain that he could not have described exploded behind his eyes.

"Stand up," Fisher Greene commanded. He tried, but his legs felt like wood stumps, disconnected from his will.

"He's too wobbly. Help him up, Antonio."

The Mexican took hold of his left shoulder and got him sitting up, then Fisher Greene stepped over and together they lifted him to his feet. Greene said, "Lean back against the wagon. It's right behind you."

Blood slid down Harvey's face from the opened scalp wound. He tilted his head so it would run down the left cheek

143

and kept it from getting into his eyes. Greene laughed. "She needs shootin' lessons. Two tries and you ain't dead yet."

What had Greene said?

"I'm disappointed we ain't gonna drown you after all, Kitren. I was looking forward to it."

The Mexican kept hold of his arm, putting a hand under his elbow and giving Harvey a little support, nodding toward the campfire, the rim of his sombrero so wide it touched Harvey's neck. The smell of smoke was in the air along with the fresh promises of the coming night. Food. They had cooked something. Would they offer any to him? He'd felt no hunger on the journey, but now his stomach twisted with need. His legs didn't like moving, but he moved them, stepping over the hateful wad of cloth in the sparse grass.

"Come on, hombre," the Mexican said. This was the one who'd met the wagon, helped dump McDonald's body in the river. Harvey knew the voice. He had to concentrate in order to stay upright, sliding one foot ahead a few inches, then sliding the other one up beside it. A very long time, it seemed, passed while they inched toward the fire. The Mexican didn't try to hurry him, in fact seemed almost gentle, compared to the treatment of the last two days. Not in this crowd, though. Nobody here was gentle. Smugglers, murderers and thieves. Those words best described the gathering.

As he struggled to walk, chills wracked him again. His teeth chattered while his face burned. Antonio called out to one of the others, who came running with a blanket off the seat of their wagon. It was dirty and stiff, but once it was wrapped around him the shivers lessened and he was able to move along with Antonio to a place close by the burning wood.

"Sit here." Harvey did as the man said, though there was nothing but the ground to sit on. Not even a rock or a log. He lay back and held the dirty blanket tighter. "You got a fever. I bring you some water. You want some water?"

He nodded his head and felt the crinkle of drying blood on his cheek. His hands and fingers still had no feeling in them. Antonio held a heavy wooden canteen steady while the wounded ranger drank from it. Harvey wondered at the unexpected kindness.

As if from a far place he heard Trey Braca yelling at the Mexicans. "Come on, come on! Get the silver loaded. I want to head back."

If the things Deke McDonald said were true, and it looked like they were, then this was a simple trade—guns for silver. The Americans wanted out of Mexico quick, and of course they had to get the treasure away from the watching eyes of Fort Duncan.

Fisher Green stood over him again. Harvey expected another boot in the face, but he heard the Mexican say, "No, no. You will kill him."

"Who cares? He won't live to Durango anyhow."

"I think he will. These devils, they are very hard men. As hard as they are cruel. You go now. My people will finish this one. I shook your hand on that. You go now."

Greene leaned down close. "Kitren? You hear me? Listen. This is what you can worry about now. Antonio here owns you. I sold you to him for a bar of silver. Like a horse or a dog. When they try you and shoot you dead, think of me." It was all the stuff of dreams. The words swept past Harvey into the darkening underbrush, but made no impression on him. He only half heard, only half understood. Greene was a giant stretched high above him, the voice coming out of shadows. Then a heavy wad of spit laced with the smell of a cigar fell on his face and mixed with the blood drying on his cheek.

CHAPTER 54

The Mexicans argued. Harvey felt confused, and not just because of the fever or the pain. Maybe he was dying after all. Shot in the chest, kicked and mauled for days, starved, he ought to be dead by now like Deke McDonald. There had been quiet for a little while after the Americans rode away. Then this loud fuss between the three men in sombreros.

One of them, a small man with a hard look on his face brought something and tried to put it in Harvey's hand. It rolled out of his fingers onto the ground. The hand was still unworkable and stiff.

"No?"

"Can't hold it." The small man shrugged and walked away.

The one called Antonio came over and sat on the ground next to Harvey. He picked up the object. "Here. You eat this." And he held it so that Harvey could bite into it. Beans wrapped in a tortilla. Harvey's jaw didn't seem to work right. He had to hold the food in his mouth and soften it, then use his tongue to break it apart and swallow. The beans hadn't been cooked enough and were hard to mash. Antonio was patient, waited til it was finished. He took the wide hat off his head and put it down beside him.

"The others are mad with me. Isidro is very quick with the knife. He would cut your throat if I allowed it. You understand why they are mad?"

Harvey didn't have the energy to answer.

"Is because I lie to the Greene man. Tell him we take you to Durango with the guns, and we judge you and put you against a wall. You understand? In my country we call the rangers from Texas, devils. And there is much hate for you.

146

"Isidro, his brother is killed by one like you, over the border for reasons nobody knows. He hates more than the rest of us. But you can never live to reach Durango, so I will find help for you. You understand?"

Harvey nodded. He felt light-headed from the fever. The words coming at him had a force of some kind, like they were solid, and bouncing off him. This could be a dream or it could be real.

"Why will I help you? I will tell you. We build for the revolution. Juarez is finishing now, and Lerdo wants his place, but he is a snake and we can not have such as that man our leader. General Diaz must be president of Mexico. These guns, these men, I and others like us will put the General into power. You understand?"

Harvey felt lost in the maze of words.

"And when we do it, we must have the friendship of the north. That is why I help you. And why I lie to the Greene man. And why Isidro and Carlos are mad with me. They don't see how I see. But I am right. I will help you, and if you live, remember what I said. Tell the others of your kind that here we are men like them, we feel pity. We are not crazy people. And before you kill the Greene man say I am sorry I had to lie."

They gave him more water, not much at a time, because it made him sick to his stomach, and he ate two tortillas without the beans. The tortillas were cold and poorly cooked. They tasted like scorched flour. True dark came on fast. The Mexicans put out their fire. The tall, skinny one the others called Carlos led a horse out of the low brush and mounted. His saddle was one of those Mexican rigs with the big saddle horn and shiny trinkets attached to the leather. They had a work team of two mules and two horses hooked to their wagon, the crates of guns hidden under canvas that looked like the sheet Harvey had lived under for two days. The knife man, Isidro, climbed aboard and held the reins ready.

Were they about to ride away and leave him? It didn't matter much. He was nearly past caring what fate had in mind. He began to believe just then that he would die out here. Antonio

147

rode a long-legged mount close and dismounted. Harvey couldn't tell the Horse's color. All the animals looked black in the young night.

"What I am thinking is if you can sit in the saddle I will ride behind you and hold you so you don't fall over. What do you think?"

What did he think? Wooden hands and fingers. Could he breathe sitting up like that? He focused on one word. "Wagon?"

"Ah, the wagon. No, is not room. And bad springs. No good. The horse better, I think."

"Where?"

"You ask where we going?" He laughed. "Not Durango."

CHAPTER 55

Getting him into the saddle was quicker and easier than Harvey expected. His legs had a little more strength in them, maybe from the tortillas and the water. His balance was no good, though, and Antonio had to hold him upright once they were ready to ride. Without the Mexican's arms around his waist, Harvey knew he'd fall off the horse. He remembered Fisher Greene telling his partner that everything out here was prickly. Not a good place to fall.

Antonio kept the horse to a slow walk. Even that was hurtful, though. With every step he felt a deep pinch among his ribs behind the bullet hole. The slug was still in there. It hadn't gone through. It was over near his right side, away from his heart, and that had to be plain luck. What had Greene said? *She* had shot him twice? And failed to kill him? The woman back at the cave. He remembered hearing her talking to Greene and Braca, though he'd never been able to understand the words or even the true sound of her voice.

He'd been right to worry about breathing. He took short inhalations and let air out without force. If he tried a deeper drag on the air it hurt too much and the muscles of his chest cramped. So he thought of breathing and wondered where they were headed.

The riders followed close behind their wagonload of guns. They were on a wide trail, going west in a straight direction instead of dodging their way through brush. He wondered if Greene and the freighter had made it away from the soldiers at Fort Duncan. Antonio must have read his thoughts. Behind him, the man said, "The two I bought you from, they have come before when no soldados live at the fort over there. I

149

think they are safe, but is Indian scouts now, too. They are ones I think you call Seminoles. The people are afraid of these Indians. They have hair long to their shoulders and seem always thinking bad things."

Harvey listened, occupied with his own misery, and made no reply.

"If those ones catch them with the silver they will steal it. I told them, I said go fast away from here while it's dark. Don't stop to camp."

Antonio was silent after that. The horses' feet brushed against grass and stones. The crates inside their wagon shifted and harness rattled. They were not far from the river. He could smell the water and hear the croak of bullfrogs.

The wagon stopped. Antonio used his spurs on his horse's flank, a touch that moved them around the wagon to a hitch rail set back a ways from the road. A dim glow spilled through a stone arch and gave shadow to the rail and the ground that circled it. Antonio slid down, keeping his hold on Harvey. The others stayed where they were.

The glow came from a lamp that nested inside a hollow in the arch. They struggled past it. There was no other light to be seen. Antonio said, "We will find him. Even priests don't sleep so soon." More stonework. A building. Doorway. It seemed very dark here. Antonio leaned Harvey against the wall and used both hands to pull open the heavy wooden door. Wood that had come from somewhere else, because trees were scarce in this part of the world. Nearly all the plants that grew out here were no taller than a man's head. There was light inside, another lamp that danced and flickered and cast shadows along the walls and floor and on the altar and cross at the back. A smell that was a mixture of smoke and perfume seemed to thicken the air..

"So, we have the light from lamps, but not the one who lights them. Do you see? I am no religious man, but I think it is like God. You understand? He light the fire and go away." Harvey had lost his sense of humor long past, but Antonio laughed at his own words.

"Is just the one old man now. I think he have a little house in the back. So here." He helped Harvey travel a dozen steps to a nearby bench and sat him down. "Lay down if you want to. I will find him." He went out the door and Harvey was alone. Sitting upright was painful, but stretching out on the long bench might be worse. Just being still helped. The pains in his chest eased a little.

"Here is your help." Harvey opened his eyes, not sure how long they'd been closed, how long he'd dozed. Flickering shadows from that one lamp had done it, a reminder of his years as a child, a small house in which nights were lit that way. He was surprised to realize he knew where his arms were. A little feeling had made its way back. He was leaning forward, his elbows on his knees for support, and he could have slept that way if they'd let him.

Antonio spoke to somebody in the Spanish language, which Harvey had never learned. Most Texans neglected it, and even anglicized and mispronounced the names of old Spanish settlements. A language and a people seen as inferior to the white settler.

The priest was old. He carried a lighted candle in a holder of some sort. Harvey felt the heat of its flame when the old man held it close, peering at his face and head. Antonio said something else, removing the blanket from around Harvey and unbuttoning his shirt. It was dried to his chest. The hole was crusted and hard with dried blood. The old man shook his head and Harvey smelled whisky or maybe tequila and realized the stumbling walk of the priest wasn't caused by the man's age.

"Is he drunk?"

"Si."

"He can't help me."

"Oh, si. He will."

CHAPTER 56

The two men got on each side of Harvey. Antonio took the candle and the two of them lifted him off the bench by his arms, which had begun to ache with the return of blood and feeling. The three of them then began to move toward the door. Harvey felt glad that Antonio was a strong man, because the old priest stumbled worse than the ranger.

It was hard to tell in uncertain light, but at first he'd thought the priest wore a hat. No, it was the way his hair was cut that made it look that way. Bald on top, then a fringe around the head, and shaved off under the fringe. Harvey thought it looked silly, but it could be just a dream and nothing to worry about.

They walked on paving stones set in the ground. His boots scraped the rough surface, but the stones were smooth and afforded sure footing. The old man holding his elbow wore a brown robe with a wide sash around it that held things together. The robe looked thick and dark and heavy, so long it brushed at his ankles, feet bare and white as fish, poking out from under the hem. A cross on a leather thong hung around the man's neck. And there was a smell about him—like the smoky perfume inside the chapel.

Another wooden doorway was set in the same sort of stone wall a short walk from the rear of the chapel. The priest opened it and motioned them inside.

"The bed," Antonio said. "He puts you in his bed."

Another lamp burned on a shelf in the corner of the tiny house. A cabin, really, one room with a fireplace and the cot they sat him on. He noted a bottle on the shelf beside the lamp, half full. The walls were made of stones like the chapel, left to form uneven clefts where shadows played. A scorpion rested on one of the rocks a few feet away, but high up near the ceiling. When Harvey was a child with Ella, the grown folks in their lives had called the little creatures stinging lizards.

The floor was made from those large, thin paving stones, like the walkway they'd used. These were trimmed square and fitted together with no spaces between. The floor could be trusted, Harvey thought. He glanced up and the scorpion had disappeared. They'd put the blanket back around his shoulders, but it wasn't enough to keep him warm. The fever seemed hotter and he shivered.

Talk peppered the air between the two men—Antonio, who'd kept him alive, and the drunk priest who might yet save him. Talk Harvey didn't understand, firing off fast as the Gatling Gun he'd seen once in the war. So fast you couldn't catch a word of it. Something was settled, though. They nodded at one another and Antonio looked solemn. The look stayed with him while he grabbed the half-full bottle off its shelf and went out the door. The priest went into a corner of his lair and came into the light with a bucket. He went out the door carrying it, the uncertain candle in his free hand.

A wind had come up. It drifted in the open doorway. Not cool, but there was life in it, and the scents of water and mud, and the brush that grew along the river. The priest almost fell as he came inside. He set the bucket down and water sloshed over its rim onto the stones of the floor. The lamp light and candle light reflected off it. Antonio came in behind him, his hands empty, the bottle probably a gift to the waiting men outside. Harvey was glad to see him back. He'd considered that Antonio might have gone for good. And that had left him feeling more alone than ever. It was a feeling he hadn't liked. It showed weakness, and Harvey had never been weak.

"This padre, he will help you now. And I will help him. There is nobody else and he is drunk."

Harvey was too weary to speak. He shook his head.

"Si, he can help you. He is many times drunk, but he knows curing things, more things than you and me know. So now you listen and you do like I say."

153

He took the blanket off Harvey's shoulders and eased him onto the narrow cot. It was a rickety affair such as might be used in a ruined army's camp. Except for the mattress. It was formed of heavy white cloth made into a bag and as he lay back on it there were sounds he remembered from corn cribs long years back. Cribs where you could play all day, crawling around in the unshucked ears, knobby and crinkly, and with a smell you could never forget.

Something wet touched his face. A wet cloth eased over his cheeks, his chin and forehead, and his scalp, cleaning away the blood and Fisher Greene's tobacco-laced spit. The heat of fever remained. And the cold that raced up and down his arms and legs and into his belly. He opened his eyes and the priest's face was close to his. Outlined by the funny looking hair. And there was more than he had guessed in that face. There was liquor of some kind, yes, with the sag of muscle and the droop of eye that came with it, but kindness, too. A little bit of a smile that caused the man to seem like he could be trusted.

Antonio leaned over him. "Your face is clean now. Like the baby bottom. The bullet that is in you, he got to come out tonight. You understand?"

"Yeah."

"First this padre says you drink this. All of it." He took the cork out of a bottle that held about a pint of something clear as water. Maybe it was water.

What choice was there? He would trust these people and hope for the best. He drank it down. The taste was bitter and green, like he'd chewed on a sprig of grass. The priest watched him drink it, took away the bottle and smiled. Antonio asked him somethng in their language, then said to Harvey, "This will help the fever. He make it from the willow and maybe from snake toes, I think."

They used the same cloth to wet his shirt over the bullet hole and soften the dried blood so that his shirt could come off. A purple and yellow bruise covered the right side of his chest. The hole, once the blood was washed away, was a sad little puckering of flesh shredded by the bullet's impact. With his upper body uncovered the chills grew worse and he began to shake more. Harvey felt helpless. There was nothing he could do for himself. If he lived or if he died, it was up to the two men standing beside his cornshuck bed. A Mexican bandit and a drunk priest.

When another strip of cloth, dry and clean, settled over his face he was thinking that if he lived and if he ever married and had kids, then grandkids, this would be a good story to tell, the kind of story kids would want to hear. He thought of Katy and wondered if he would ever see her again. He breathed a sharp odor through the cloth. Why was this thing over his face? What were they doing? It smelled like...what? Rubbing Alcohol? Kerosene? Tequila? What? He hadn't been on a whisky drunk in many a year, but it was like this. Like this before you passed out. Antonio had said something about snake toes a little while ago. Snakes didn't have toes. It was a funny thing to say. He almost laughed out loud, but instead he floated away.

CHAPTER 57

Harvey brought a hand up and wiped at the itch in his hair. It felt rough, and he remembered that the doctor back in Stampede had sewed it up after—after something. He opened his eyes and saw the same scorpion, or one just like it, on that same rock that was part of the wall beside the bed he lay on. He looked at his hand and moved his fingers and they hurt. He looked around the room and was alone. He raised his other arm and moved the fingers of that hand, and it hurt him again. His hands felt stiff and wooden, but he could feel again, and he knew where he was, and why, and looked down at his chest where the bullet had hit him.

A wide white cloth was wrapped around him, tight and clean except for the pink stain where it covered the bullet hole. It hurt to breathe still, but only a little, not like before. His head ached. He reached up to feel again of the rough spot, and identified stitches where Fisher Greene's boot had opened the wound.

Where had they gone? The priest? Antonio? He looked around again, and noticed for the first time that one wall held a window, an open square with the shutters folded back and daylight coming in. So he'd slept all night. Did this mean he was going to live after all? It might. It surely might mean that. He closed his eyes and slept a little longer until the door slammed shut and woke him a second time.

Three people, a crowd inside the cramped space. The priest, who moved with a steadier walk now, so was not drunk, a woman, a large woman, holding a wooden tray with two plates on it and if he was not dreaming, also a cup with hot coffee in it by the smell. And a girl, a child, no more than eight or ten, with long pigtails and a scowl on her face.

"Buenas dias," the priest said. He raised the cross that hung around his neck and kissed it, then put a hand over the pink stain. His lips moved but no words came out. Then he spoke to the girl. The big woman stood waiting.

"They make me come tell you," the girl said, standing at the foot of the bed, "He take the bullet from you." She pointed to the priest. The old man reached into a fold of his robe and brought out a mangled piece of lead. He laid it on Harvey's chest. So that's what was working around in his ribs all this time. He brought a hand to it, fingers stiff and nearly immovable, but managed to grasp it and stuff it into a pants pocket.

"How come you speak my language?"

The question drew a smile to her lips that didn't last long. "At school we learn."

"Tell him I say thanks."

She nodded and rattled off something and the others nodded their heads, too.

"What was that stuff they put me to sleep with last night? Can you ask him that?"

She spoke to the priest again and he knelt down beside the bed and brought out a corked bottle. Faded letters on the label spelled *ether.* He put it back under the bed and stood up.

The girl stepped closer and lowered her voice. "If he have no tequila he smell it and sleep. We all know this."

Harvey remembered seeing a bottle just like it in a confederate medical tent years before. This priest could use some supervision.

"Tell him there's a scorpion on his wall." He glanced up, and it was still sitting there.

She spoke with the priest again while the big woman stood holding her tray.

"He knows about the scorpion, sir. He is Franciscan, and sometimes preaches to it at night, as Saint Francis would."

They could use this one at the Stampede church. Loosen things up. "Where is Antonio?"

"I don't know, sir."

"The wagon? Is it still outside?"

She looked confused and glanced around the room. "Nobody else is here." The priest must have sensed what Harvey was asking. He said something to the girl.

"Your friend is gone sir. And soon now the soldiers come from the fort. He has sent them word of you."

He'd liked that man. It hurt a little to think he'd never see him again, but that was the case and he was on his own again. He had liked Deke, too, but Deke McDonald's body was floating toward the Gulf and the men who did that had to be dealt with. He felt grateful to be alive, but there was plenty of trouble ahead, and him only half himself.

The room contained no chairs, but along a wall sat a bench long enough for two narrow people to cluster side by side, and a rickety table barely big enough to hold the tray the big woman put down on it. One of the table legs was loose and had to be brought back to its upright position when she carried it over and put it down beside the bed.

Harvey said, "Thank you very much." She paid him no attention and went out the door without a word to any of them. The girl followed, but before she disappeared she gave him a quick smile and said, "You are welcome."

The priest helped him sit up and held onto him til the room stopped spinning and he was able to stay upright. He was like the little table, needed help to function. There was something else he was surprised about, but had not remembered til now. It was the chills, the fever, the sense of living inside a crazy dream, and all of that was gone. He'd slept it off. Maybe the bitter water he drank last night had helped.

He was able to hold the cup. The coffee in it was nearly cold, but he didn't care. The plates held refried beans and tortillas. His jaw still bothered him, but the beans were cooked soft and the tortillas were tender and tasted just right.

After he ate, the priest held his arms while he sank back onto the cornshuck mattress. The maneuver took the strain off his middle, off the bullet wound that he hoped had begun to heal. He thought it a pity that language stood between them as a wall. The old fellow was a strange one, and a long hard life was written in the wrinkles of his face. He would have stories to tell. Some true, some not, but they would make good listening.

The shirt they'd peeled off him last night was nowhere to be seen. He didn't miss the shirt—it was ruined anyhow, but there'd been a sack of tobacco in the pocket, and his badge as well. He hadn't thought about a smoke in days, but wanted one badly now, likely because it wasn't available. The priest had been simply standing near the bed, watching him, looking like he wanted to talk, as Harvey did, both men knowing it couldn't be accomplished.

Knuckles rapped at the door and it swung back to let in two more strangers. These were soldiers, from the fort, he guessed. The youngest wore the bars of a first lieutenant, his cap held under an arm and dark hair topping a freckled face. His movements were smooth and precise, a man used to square corners and the parade ground. A few steps behind him another one with sergeant stripes on his sleeve came along slower, age in his face and step.

The officer spoke to Harvey. "Sir, I'm Lieutenant Gordon. This is Sergeant Moreland. We're here to take you across to the Fort Duncan dispensary."

"I'm grateful to see you, Lieutenant." He noticed that his voice sounded weak, like he'd heard it before coming from old men. Wheezy and thin.

"What is your name, sir?"

The old priest reached inside his habit and brought out the badge and Harvey's tobacco sack. He handed them to the young officer.

"Oh? We weren't told you were a ranger."

"Kitren's the name. How'd you know I was here?"

"A young boy. Little fellow. Came at daybreak with this note." He handed the ragged piece of paper to Harvey.

The message was printed in block letters with a broken lead. It read, "Come for the wounded Texan at the old church over the river. Goodbye from Antonio." A last gesture from the

159

Mexican who had saved his life. How lucky Harvey had been. What a friend Antonio had been. Him and this old worn-out ether-sniffing priest.

CHAPTER 58

At a gesture from the officer Sergeant Moreland stepped forward and offered a hand. "Can you walk, mister? You think?"

"I don't know." He let the soldier pull him up, then stood. He managed one step, but the room swirled around his head and he felt suddenly sick to his stomach. He backed up and sat down again. "Maybe not." The sergeant turned on his heel and went out the door. A minute later he was back carrying a rolled-up stretcher, two poles and canvas. He unrolled the apparatus and laid it on the floor.

"We'll get you out with this."

Harvey was able to slide from the bed to his knees, then roll himself onto the canvas. Sergeant Moreland bent down and took hold of one end, waiting for the others to help. The lieutenant stood his ground, holding badge and tobacco sack and waited until the priest stepped forward and grabbed hold. Getting through the door was the worst part of it. He thought for a while they were about to drop the stretcher, or tilt it so that he fell off. Neither happened.

As they carried him along the stone walk he could see that the walls of the old church were built of river rock, rounded and smoothed by the Rio Grande current over uncounted ages. He wondered how many scorpions lived in the wall and what the priest said to them when he preached. The air smelled fresh and clean. Harvey thought quietly—"I'm still alive. Still alive. And that's enough for now."

He rode propped on the seat of a one-horse buggy, Sergeant Moreland beside him. Lieutenant Gordon rode along with them, his mount a spirited gray gelding that shied at birds when

161

they flew into his path. The sun was straight overhead by the time a ferry carried them across the river, wide at this point, with roiling currents around them hurrying from their beginnings in the mountains and valleys of Colorado and New Mexico to the Gulf and the Atlantic Ocean. This must be the crossing that Greene and Braca had intended using before they learned about the soldiers.

"How much longer?" Harvey asked as the buggy ground its way onto Texas soil. More blood had leaked from his bullet wound, staining the dressing a darker red. It hurt, and he felt tired. His head ached. That kick from Fisher Greene had left a hurt that had not let up since.

"Not long. We most there." Harvey glanced up and saw the flagpole supporting what he figured was the stars and stripes. Too far to tell. The pole itself looked like a toothpick in the distance.

"Doctor there?"

The old sergeant turned his head and looked at him. "Medic feller. He's all right. We got some doctor coming, but he ain't here yet. We just come back. Fort's been vacant a long time."

Gordon rode close and leaned down. "Sergeant, I'm going ahead. Let them know we're coming. Drive him right up to the hospital building. I'll have somebody waiting."

"Yes, sir."

A quick spur in his flank sent the gray off at a gallop. Harvey watched them go and considered that the young man wore a uniform and sat on an army saddle, but for a second or two he was just a kid having a little fun. Watching the gray run brought up the memory of his own pony that had carried him over many a mile only to lie dead because of Harvey's failure. Failure to pay close attention. It was a memory with him now for the rest of his life. A sorrow to carry.

162

CHAPTER 59

The fort was a scattered group of buildings, all erected with the stone that was used for just about everything out here. That and adobe. It all looked solid and well-built. A handsome collection.

"We been hard at work since we got in," Moreland said. "Things had fell apart some, nobody here to take care of it." There was a gathering of uniforms outside one of the buildings. "Mess hall over there. We get you inside I'll go fetch something for you."

Gordon stood beside an open door that looked fresh-painted. An older officer, nearer Sergeant Moreland's age, stood beside him. Harvey saw the gleam of a colonel's insignia on the man's uniform. "That there's Colonel Walter with the lieutenant. Commander of the fort."

Moreland brought the buggy to a halt. He climbed down from his seat and began to haul out the stretcher. Both officers stepped down from the porch and approached Harvey. He hadn't yet tried to move, and dreaded doing it. "Sir, this is my commander, Colonel Walter."

The colonel removed his hat and reached to shake Harvey's hand. He looked like a better fed version of the sergeant Harvey had come in with. "How are you feeling, Ranger?"

"Wore down a little, I reckon. Ready for a bed."

"We'll get you inside the hospital and fix you up. You're the first patient from outside the fort, matter of fact. And the only one for now." Moreland spread the stretcher and took one end of it. Walter turned to the lieutenant and said, "Help him with that, Gordon."

Their voices echoed inside the near-empty building, as did their footsteps on the stone floor. A cot stood ready and it was

163

a great relief to Harvey when he was able to stretch his legs and lie back on what felt like a feather pillow. "Much obliged," he said. "Much obliged."

Moreland headed for the mess hall. The officers stood above him, interested and wanting to talk. Harvey didn't mind the interest but doubted he'd be able to converse with the men right now. His chest and throat felt dry and unresponsive.

Walter said, "Lieutenant Gordon tells me you suffered a gunshot wound that a priest over there treated you for."

"Yeah. Took the bullet out."

"I have a medic on duty. He'll be along in a little while to check you over. Pity you couldn't make it here sooner."

"Couldn't be helped."

The colonel looked undecided, then seemed to make a decision. "Sergeant Moreland will bring you some food and drink in a while. We'll let you rest for now and have our own lunch. Maybe we can talk a bit later in the day. I'll need the details of what happened to you."

He watched the two men walk out the door and close it behind them. It was only a room that he was alone in, but it felt like the whole world was empty except for his tired and aching body. He'd have to lay it all out for Walter. It wouldn't happen that way except for the wound. Unwounded he'd break away to Austin and report in to Ranger headquarters. Still, it was a fine thing that the soldiers were here. Not long ago he was expecting to drown in the river at the hateful hands of Fisher Greene. It was hard right now to feel grateful, but he was. He knew he was.

He'd begun to doze off to sleep when Moreland came back carrying a tray of food. The smell of it woke him. He felt starved. There were biscuits and ham and for the third time lately, beans. These were pintos, and he didn't mind. His jaw still closed with clicks and his teeth didn't quite meet, but he ignored all that and just ate. There was no coffee, but a tall glass of clean, clear water, and that was plenty good enough. Finished at last, he lay back and burped and said, "Thanks Sergeant. You eat?"

"In a minute. You want a smoke?" He gestured at the tobacco sack and Ranger badge that Gordon had left on the floor at the foot of the cot.

"Yeah. Can't roll one. Fingers don't work good."

The sergeant had one ready and between Harvey's lips in a few seconds. A scratch of a match across the wooden cot frame and it was lit. "I'll roll one for myself, you don't mind."

There was nowhere to sit. Moreland backed up to the wall nearby and slid down to the floor, his back against stone. They smoked in silence for a while. "I seen that note the Lieutenant had."

"Yeah?"

"That name. Antonio. He the one shot you?"

"Oh, no. He saved me. Hauled me to the church where they got the bullet out."

"So you know him, do you?" Moreland talked like he was advancing on a point.

"Wouldn't say that, no."

"There's one named Antonio Flores over there. I know because he's one of them we watch for at the crossing. Bandit, killer. Doing that whole Mexican revolution thing you hear about. If that's who sent the note you're plenty lucky he didn't slice your throat for you."

"Where's he from, the Flores fellow?"

"Durango, I think. They say he's building up his own little army there."

"No, couldn't be this one. He talked about his family down in Oaxaca."

Moreland carried both cigarette butts with him when he left. "You know how the army is. Everything neat and clean. Twenty years now, and it has been a severe clash with my nature."

The meal had helped. He felt stronger, or thought so anyhow, with no way to test it, and no inclination, either. The empty sense of loneliness had eased. He thought about what the sergeant had said. So Antonio was a bandit and a cutthroat, was he? Or so it was told. He felt some resentment at the

165

description, glad he'd thought to discredit the man's identity. All of that was somebody else's problem. He'd go on believing help had come in unlikely form from unexpected kindness.

CHAPTER 60

The door opened. "Afternoon, sir. How you feeling?" The man was near Harvey's age, early forties probably. Blue eyes nested like shiny bird eggs between a heavy mop of blond hair and a beard of the same color that hung halfway down his chest. He wore a white smock. A pipe was fixed in his nearly-hidden mouth. He carried a notebook in one hand and a cowhide-bottomed straight chair in the other. Not one of the soldiers.

"Who're you?"

"My name? It's Abbot. Jeffrey Abbot, if you must know." Somewhere within the beard Harvey thought the man smiled. The visitor parked his chair beside the cot and sat down and crossed his legs. Instead of boots he had what looked like Indian moccasins on his feet. He opened the notebook and brought a pencil from somewhere. "Tell me how you're feeling."

"Hard to say. My head hurts bad where I got shot and then lately kicked. The bullet hole stings when I move. My hands can't feel much and my fingers barely work." Abbot wrote in his notebook.

"They told me there was no doctor here."

The man looked up from his writing, but kept the pencil poised. "I'm not. I'm just here til one of their army docs is posted to the fort. But don't worry. I won't do you any harm." He took the pipe from his mouth with his free hand and chuckled at his own words.

"Just to reassure you, I spent many years assisting a regimental surgeon during the late war. Mustered out and been training since. I'm almost a doctor."

"A sober one."

"Excuse me?" They spent some time on the details of how Harvey came to be here and how he took on the wounds and the aches.

Abbot looked closely at Harvey's scalp. "I'll say this—drunk or sober, someone did a good job restitching it." He put away the pencil and laid the notebook on the floor. "I'll need you to stand up now and let's get your boots and pants off. I want to put some sulphur on your scalp and chest."

"You're gonna have me lay up here naked?"

Abbot clenched the pipe between his teeth again and talked around it. "No, I've got a gown for you. And I'll send the pants out to a laundry detail. No offense, but you could use some soap and water yourself."

Harvey had endured it before at times in his life, but had never learned to enjoy the smell of sulphur. The stink leaked out from the fresh bandage around his torso, tighter this time in case a rib was cracked, and as yet unstained by blood. And it drifted down off his head. Abbot had smeared a salve on him that was fortified with the stuff and said there was no evidence of bad infection. The chills and fever hadn't come back. The medic had decided, after poking on him and listening to his heart and his lungs, that he was about to pull through the whole affair. A week on this cot, staring at the ceiling, and another few taking life slow and easy, and he could go back to being himself again.

What then? That was the question, all right. The unfinished hunt for Ella's killer, now this thing he'd stumbled across. Raines and his bunch. Ella came first. He would never stop til somebody paid for what they'd done to her. That was personal. This other was legal business. Ranger business. The Mexicans could get Raines for hauling guns over the border, but he was safe from them as long as he stayed put. And once he had the silver on this side of the Rio Grande there was no law to stop him.

But murder. That was a different story. Deke McDonald was dead at the hands of Greene and Braca, on the orders of Raines.

And Harvey himself had seen it happen. He was the key to prosecuting them all for murder. Right now they thought he was dead, and none of them could guess that retribution was on its way.

The day was shutting down. A bugle sounded mess call. Sunlight fed through a west-facing window with a beam sharp and straight as an arrow against the wall near Harvey's head. He imagined soldier boys in blue uniforms lining up for their supper, officers like Gordon and Walter sitting down to table in their own private room. He'd never understood that—the lather of privilege on a few and the lack of it on the rest. Wasn't that way in the Rangers. Captains ate with their men, lived or died with them. That's how it ought to be.

Sergeant Moreland brought him another tray with his supper on it. Abbot had left the chair, and it made a good resting spot for the collection. He'd also brought along an empty tin can from the kitchen. "Got you something for your ashes now. You can smoke all you want to."

"Thank you, Sergeant. You've been good to me." He sat up, this time unaided, and put his feet on the floor.

"That's a mighty pretty gown you got on, sir."

CHAPTER 61

The medic showed up again just as darkness began, with a burning candle and a little round table that he set it on. He asked Harvey how he felt and got back a pleasing answer, though the patient neglected to mention boredom, which had become the greater truth. Abbot retrieved the badge where it had lain since arrival. He looked around and then pinned it to the side of the mattress. Lit by the uncertain candle flame it winked like a flirting eye. "Army likes things neat. Colonel's on his way over."

Another bugle call lifted itself not far away. One Harvey recognized as Taps. They'd be taking down the flag out in front of the the fort now, folding it and putting it away for the night. It had a lonesome feel to it, that sound did. You hear it and you find yourself remembering all the reasons for sadness. It ended on a long, drawn-out note that was answered by a pack of coyotes hunting the thorny hillside for their own supper.

"I don't see a reason to stay in here tonight, or detail anybody for the job. So you'll be alone. There's guards out, of course, so yell if you need help." Colonel Walter and Lieutenant Gordon came through the open door, followed by an Indian who wore army britches and a colorful shirt of red and blue that hung down outside the waist. And, as Antonio had described, had long hair down to his shoulders and a look on his face like he was thinking bad thoughts.

The Colonel dismissed Abbot with a silent nod and waited til the door shut. "I'd like to hear your story if you feel strong enough."

Harvey told it all again.

"Since you represent the government we ought to inform your superiors of your situation. Austin, I presume?"

170

"That's a long ride."

"These men can handle a long ride." He indicated Gordon and the Indian. "I brought them over tonight thinking already that they'd be needed."

"Well, sir, nobody in Austin's concerned about me just now. Far as they know I'm still in Stampede on a leave of absence looking into my sister's death." It bothered him to say it that way, like Ella was at a distance instead of wrapped around his heart.

"Oh. Sorry to hear that. Recently?"

"Yeah."

"And is that a part of what you've just been through, or separate altogether?"

"I don't know, Colonel. It didn't seem so at first, but I'm starting to wonder. It's your business what you do, but I'd rather the lieutenant here make a shorter ride to that little town. It's north of here a day's travel."

Walter glanced at his junior officer with an inquiring look. Gordon nodded and eyed the scout who went on thinking his thoughts. In the candlelight the Indian's face could have been carved from firewood. Dark face and hands, almost black. Antonio had said the Indian scouts here were Seminoles. Harvey knew a little about them. From the Florida swamp country, they had mingled with runaway slaves and made new lives in that protective place.

"Who should they see there?"

Good question. He considered. "Blacksmith at the stable. Name of Caudel. There's others I don't want knowing I'm alive. I'll give you a list." Gordon found paper and pencil and wrote the names down. Harvey didn't mention Katy Wallace, but it was her face and name that stood out in his mind, the one he couldn't stop missing.

The three men prepared to leave. Walter said, "Shall I snuff the candle?"

"Thanks, no. I'll put it out myself. I like the shadows jumping around the wall. Keeps me company." He remembered something else. "Lieutenant, there's another thing

171

I wish you'd do." He told them about Deke McDonald's white dog and drew a simple map on Gordon's paper.

CHAPTER 62

Jeffrey Abbot, the medic, dosed him daily with a new smearing of sulphured salve and a fresh bandage. Not any enjoyment in it, but truth was, it must be helping him. There'd been no more infection, and by Thursday blood had stopped seeping through the bandage. He knew it was Thursday because he asked the bearded man.

"I can put a calendar in here if you'd like."

"That's accomodating of you, but I can keep up from here." The headache remained, but it was lessening.

Sergeant Moreland continued bringing food at mess times and often stayed to share a smoke from the nearly-empty sack of tobacco. "I got two in my footlocker," he said. "I'll bring you one for payback." The sergeant also carried out Harvey's bedpan and brought it back washed and clean. He didn't seem to mind, but Harvey hated the idea of another man doing such as that for him. Like many things lately, though, it was necessary and the old soldier seemed to do it without resentment.

Friday morning brought clouds and some light rain that he could hear on the roof. He woke to the sound and felt dread at the thought that another day was here to be endured. The headache was much better this morning, though, a small blessing. Without moving, he knew somehow that he was stronger, and went through the process of standing to prove it. The dressing from the day before was still unmarked by blood. That had to be a good sign. He'd slept right through reveille, but didn't mind it, and considered that he wouldn't mind never hearing it again.

It felt good to stand for a while after being down so long. His legs were clumsy, but he paced the room and they slowly loosened up. He stood by the open window looking out at the world he wanted to get back to. He'd need to revisit Raines's cave on the way back if there was a way he could slip in unseen. His gunbelt might still be there where they left it. And his Colt .45. He remembered the feel of it in his hand. And thought about the feel of Fisher Greene's boots.

Abbot unwrapped the bandage in the middle of the day, just before the sergeant brought in his lunch. Harvey felt like the soldier was probably tired of waiting on him, and resentful of it, but he never let on if he was.

Moreland said, "Last time I seen your bare skin you was purple as a muskadine." The color had faded to a streaky yellow now. Not a pretty sight, but he was healing. The sulphur stink bloomed around the bed where Abbot performed the ritual. The soldier said, "I'll go on now and come back for the bowl and stuff after while." He tipped his hat and went out. A hot cup of coffee had come with it this time, and the scent of it mingled with the scent of the salve to create a new odor that was not all that appetizing.

The clean bandage was wrapped tight around his chest. Abbot said, "I'm not sure about those ribs, but if one or two are cracked they ought to heal back okay. You just need to keep yourself wrapped good so they don't move around. And try to stay out of fistfights."

"That's my plan. How long?"

"To heal up? Oh, I'd venture a month or so, you ought to be fine. You'll be able to tell for yourself just by how it feels to move around."

"I'll tell you, doc, I'm lucky to be here. You are greasing a grateful man."

The medic stood up with a stifled groan and adjusted the unlit pipe that seemed to precede him everywhere. He took Harvey's tray off the floor and set it on the straight chair, then slid it closer to the bed. "Could use more furniture in here, wouldn't you say?"

"No complaints from this one." Alone finally, he tried the coffee first. It had cooled, as had the bowl of stew and the cornbread, but it was tasty enough to suit him. Compared to floating face-down in the Gulf Of Mexico it was, in fact, perfect. The door opened and he heard footsteps and figured it was Sergeant Moreland coming back to share a smoke and a conversation. He took another bite of stew meat.

"Harvey?"

Of course not. That was impossible. His feelings had made him hear what was not there. That had to be it. He looked up and tried to deny the sight, but yes it was. It was true.

Katy Wallace said, "How are you?"

CHAPTER 63

Everything in him, everything but his body itself, jumped from the bed and ran to her. His mind seemed to tumble as if he'd leaped off a high point into the warm water of a swimming hole.

"...what?..." It was all he could manage.

"Am I doing here?" She came closer, knelt beside him and took the bowl and spoon from his hands. He swallowed that last bite of food and she was so close he could smell the rain in her hair despite the salve. She wore it in the single braid that he liked so much, the way she'd worn it the first time he ever saw her. She put her arms around him.

"They said you nearly died."

"...Yeah. I..." She'd come through the desert brush, wore a man's shirt and pants with rips in them, like you got riding in this country. Her face was scratched with the thin, shallow slice of mesquite and cholla thorns. Tiny beads of blood had dried on her cheeks.

"Don't be mad," she said. "Cee didn't want me to come, but I told them I was coming anyway."

"She threatened to ride alone." Cee Tims had stepped inside. Harvey stopped trying to figure it out. The artist looked grim. There was a little blood on his face, too, from scratches. "Lieutenant Gordon said Deke is dead."

Harvey looked away from Katy and nodded his head. His throat felt paralyzed.

"Are you sure?"

"Oh, yes." He found his voice after all. "They beat him so bad...threw him in the river."

Tims shoved his hands in his pockets and stood there quietly. He'd known it already, but hearing Harvey's surety hit him hard, anyway.

"Sorry to tell it. I know he was your friend."

"Friend, yes. Fine detective. We worked together a long time."

"You Pinkerton, too?"

Tims nodded. "I can guess who killed him, but can you name them?"

That's how it was, then. There'd been two of them all along, working together. "Greene and Braca. Taking orders from Raines. There's a woman, too. I never saw her. She's the one shot me, killed my horse. I think she's the same one took a bead on me outside the cafe. Can't figure who she is."

"Your pony's alive," the girl said.

He couldn't change the direction of the belief he'd carried for days. Katy smiled, and her eyes were wet, but he knew she was wrong.

"I was there. The horse died under me."

Cee Tims said, "Katy's right. Ed Caudel has him at the stable. He's hurt, but he'll recover, same as you. He showed up at the stable Monday, bleeding from a flank, and of course we knew something bad had happened to you. I rode out to Deke's place with Ed, couldn't find any trace of you or Deke, but somebody shut Ada up in the cabin. He was wounded too, though he survived it."

He was starting to feel like he was in the middle of a dream, or a miracle. The pony lived. One less guilt he had to carry. "The dog? It was me put him there. Left a little food and water. I asked the lieutenant to stop off and see about him. Reckon they judged me crazy with the cabin empty. I figured Deke would want to save him if we could. That his name? Ada?"

"Adahy. Cherokee name."

He said, "You a Pinkerton too, Katy?" It was a prickly thing to ask, but if she was, and if she'd carried him along on pretense...

"Oh, god no. First I knew, Cee told me on the ride down here." She paused and he saw understanding in her eyes and thought he'd probably offended her again. "I'm just who I told you I am. For good or bad."

CHAPTER 64

Moreland came for the dishes. He said, "Lieutenant's in with the Colonel right now. They'll be in to talk to you pretty soon. Meantime, there's a meal laid out for you folks in the officer's mess. I'll take you over there."

Cee told him, "I'd rather eat with the enlisted men." That raised him a notch or two in Harvey's estimation.

The sergeant offered his lazy smile. "I understand your thinking, sir, but the Colonel is big on genteel hospitality. He'll be offended if you turn it down."

Harvey expected Katy to leave him then and follow the men out the door. Instead she said, "Bring me something, Cee. I'm not leaving here." Then, as hard as it was to imagine, he was alone with the woman he'd thought about all these days. What would he say to her? His chest began to ache a little and he lay back on his pillow. What would she say to him?

"Damn you, Harvey Kitren. I ride through thorns to get to you, and next thing I know you're still trying to make me out a liar. And don't try to pussyfoot out of it. Always poking at me, looking for something to hold against me. Like just now. *You a Pinkerton too?* If that poor mare Ed loaned me was not so tired I believe I'd just ride on back to Stampede this minute."

She stood up and walked to the window. She put her attention on the river far below the fort. "We brought you some clothes. Rosa found your coat in your room and sent it along. The lieutenant said you needed them."

The worst of it was, she was exactly right. He was always poking, nearly hoping, he realized, to find something...something he could use—for what? Why, to use the way they used stone to build this fort. Stack one reason on top of the other and pretty soon you've got a wall that separates yourself from the fact that you love a woman. Pretty soon you've got your own private little fort and you're safe. Harvey decided just then he'd been safe too long.

"I love you, Katy." And his next thought was, *who said that?*

She turned away from the window, but there was no surrender in the look of her. There were only the two of them in the room, so he knew with certainty he'd been the one who spoke the scary words.

"I know that, Harvey. But if you ever want to hear the same from me you'd better get to adding something."

He thought of how it would be, what a sad thing it would be, if she went back to Stampede like this. But what was it he ought to say now? She was impatient. It wouldn't wait for tomorrow.

"I'm sorry, Katy. I won't doubt you again."

"Never? You'd better be sure about that."

"Never." And it was going to be all right now, because she had the beginnings of a smile on her face. She came close again, and she was tender towards him in ways he'd needed without knowing it for a very long time.

CHAPTER 65

He found his gunbelt and Colt right where he'd expected. Striking another match, he looked around the dark space to see what else might be there. Nothing he could see. The belt and pistol had been tossed against the wall and had fallen into a twisted pile obscured by a turn in the cavern wall. He remembered they'd loaded everything, including himself and Deke, in a great hurry, anxious to leave. They hadn't taken the time to search. Probably never even thought about the gun again. He was, after all, slated to die.

"Find it?" Cee Tims had followed him part way into the opening and stood waiting.

"Yeah. Still here." He brought it out into the light. The belt was scuffed and dirty, and he'd have to clean the Colt. Looked like dirt in the barrel. Finding it gave him a good feeling. One more thing that fell on the right side of things. One more he could add to that pretty woman standing by a tree waiting for him.

He said, "No point gong by Deke's place, is there?"

"Can't think of any." Cee went on, "Caudel's got the dog. Coons probably ate the chickens by now. I wish there was something we could do for poor Deke, but there's not. Besides, we need to get you out of sight. Don't want Raines or any of his people spotting you. Spoil the surprise."

Harvey had to wait for a boost from the other man when he mounted the horse they'd brought for him. Another mare, this one a roan with a swayed back under a worn-down saddle, that Cee and Katy had delivered on the end of a lead rope. Still, Ed Caudel had loaned the animal like the friend he was.

Katy climbed into her own saddle with the sort of grace she always showed, wearing the man clothes she'd had on the week

181

before. Cleaner now, because she'd brought along a couple of dresses for the few days they'd waited, and the always helpful Sergeant Moreland had passed them along to a laundry detail. You had to admire the army. From a distance.

They'd circled east off the regular trail in order to pass far from the Double R headquarters. And kept a careful eye on the countryside ahead lest they come on wranglers working at their job. Their timing was good. The sun dropped past the western horizon before they reached town, and nobody saw them ride in.

Harvey's bay pony stood in the outside pen with another half dozen animals and the three they added to the mix. He allowed the ranger's hand on his neck and on the crusted wound in his hindquarters. Caudel had covered it with worm medicine, and that might be all that could be done except wait for time to fix it. "What about the dog?" He asked.

Cee told him, "Shut up inside. He'll be all right." Their voices got threatening barks from somewhere toward the back of the building.

Harvey said, "Strong enough to bark that loud, he ought to pull through, huh?"

They walked along the sandy street and took the alley beside the general store past the water well to the back door of Morgan Bailey's house.

Cee Tims went on to his own room. Katy lit a lamp and stayed to help Harvey shuck his boots and climb into the bed. Their landlady peeped inside. "Heard y'all clomping around. Is this Lazarus, up from the grave?"

"And glad of it," Harvey said. He was tired, and many of his aches and pains were still with him, but the headache was gone and he felt stronger. His hands had most of the feeling back in them and his fingers worked like always. "I missed this bed."

"You want a bite? I've got leftovers still warm."

"Believe I would like that. Missed your cooking, too. Want me to come to the table?"

Katy said, "You stay where you are. I'll bring it."

Morgan Bailey grinned at Katy and said, "Well, now. What have we here?" And followed Katy to the kitchen.

CHAPTER 66

When he'd finished, as Katy gathered the plate and cup and fork he'd used, he said, "You go rest. I'll be fine tonight. And one more favor, if you don't mind. In the morning ask Dave Mikeska to come see me."

She bent down and kissed his forehead. "Your wish will be granted."

"You're still a sassy woman."

"And what else?"

"And fine looking."

"There's more."

He gave up. "And I think highly of you?"

"All right, Harvey. You're coming along. I'm nearly convinced.Goodnight."

Mikeska knocked on his door next morning a little while after the clock in the parlor struck nine. He came inside carrying a cup of coffee. "Morgan sent this," he said.

"Thanks, Dave. That woman is about half angel." He propped himself up on the pillow and drank from the cup. "Appreciate you coming. Have a seat." Mikeska picked the stuffed chair and eased himself down. Harvey said, "Where's your boss these days?"

"I'm not real sure. Him and Braca came back from their trip, wherever they went. Must've been a week ago. He was around a while, long enough to find fault with the saloon and us that work the place, like always. Braca keeps a room there when he's in town, and they stayed for a couple of nights and left on another run somewhere. I never heard their destination."

"Where do they keep Braca's wagon? At the stable?"

"Sometimes. But this go-round he left it behind the saloon, right on the river bank. I thought it was a funny place to leave it."

"You see what's in it?"

"I never thought to look. Braca's a feisty character. I stay clear of him and his business. Why?"

Harvey didn't answer the question. "Has Greene got a girlfriend, somebody that hangs around him when he's in town?"

Mikeska thought about it. "I ain't certain about that. He likes the ladies, I reckon you know it well as I do. I know he visits that house yonder from time to time. And there's two women work the bar sometimes, and live upstairs. But a girlfriend...I don't know."

"If a woman was to come on a visit at night would she have to come through the saloon and go upstairs?"

"Oh, no. There's a back stair goes up to the second and third floors. They put it in so anybody has a room up there can come and go without having to work their way past all the card players and drunks."

"Here's my impression of you, Dave. You work for Raines and Greene, but you're not exactly a friend of theirs. You're not a man would go talking about me being back in this bed alive. Would that be right?"

Mikeska shifted in the chair. "You ain't got to worry. I never knew much anyway, about what happened, except you hadn't come back from a ride. Never heard talk from anybody except the folks here, at the dinner table. They was all concerned. Me, too, of course. And I had my suspicions you mighta tangled with Greene someplace. I didn't bring it up when he come back. I ain't his pal. Nor is anybody I know of."

"Just leave me out of the conversation is what I'm asking."

"Fisher do this to you?"

"I'll tell all when I write my life story, Dave. But he's a good man to stay clear of. And one more thing—you know that cowhand name of Luther Welty? From the Double R?"

"Everybody knows Luther."

185

"Why is that?"

"Always out for a good time, that boy, drunk or sober."

"I can't seem to locate him. Heard he'd gone up to Abilene."

"Well...now I think about it, Luther ain't been around in a while."

"If you hear anything about him I'd love to share in it."

Mikeska said he'd be sure to do that and stood to leave. "I'll take that cup back to Morgan if you finished with it." Harvey looked down and saw that it was empty. He handed it over.

He felt like the man had been truthful. Dave was a gladhander and the kind who'd take the easy road when he could, but Harvey hadn't noted any of the tells that exposed lies, the mannerisms you looked for when you questioned a suspect. Anyhow, Fisher Greene was not in town, which meant he and the freighter had hauled Raines's silver to a buyer in another location. With any luck they wouldn't be back for a while yet.

And the Welty boy. He doubted there'd be any luck in that direction. He wasn't even certain what it was he wanted from Luther except to go over that night again with him—listen closer, because there was something.

CHAPTER 67

For three more days he was mostly still, kept to the bed while Morgan and Katy took turns wrapping bandage around his chest.

Doctor William Pruett, who'd first stitched up his scalp a while back showed up carrying a black bag and judged the new stitches as good as his own. Harvey was a little aggravated that his landlady had fetched the man.

Pruett put away his stethoscope and said, "No worry. I'll keep it to myself. They're concerned about you is all. I can tell 'em now that you're just fine. And still lucky. That bullet could have meant the end for you, but you were turned just right so it missed your vitals."

He began to believe nothing was cracked. The old familiar pains didn't appear when he got up for the privy, as he did now and then, refusing to allow anybody to carry out his chamber pot. He'd had more than enough of that kind of help. The yellow streaks across his chest faded and the bullet hole was becoming a puckered scar. Ed Caudel came visiting, clean and dressed up in Sunday garb, just to see for himself that Harvey was back from the brink and deliver the pint of Neatsfoot Oil Katy had asked him for.

"You don't object, I think I'll keep that dog. Don't know where the man found him, but I've been told he's a Pyrenees; herd dog from somewhere overseas."

"He don't belong to me. I just give him some water."

"Answers to that Indian name Cee told me, but I don't care for it much. Since you don't have a claim on him, I'll try to think up a new one to suit myself."

Ed had come walking back from the church house with Rosa, the woman on her twice-weekly pilgrimage across the field.

Caudel wanted to say something. He started, hesitated, then began again. "I talked to the people over there again."

"The church?"

"About the cemetery."

"I have not been to see yet. Anybody mess with Ella?"

"No. It's like you saw it last. But it worries me. There's always some self-important fool will go against good sense."

"Especially them that dress up for Sunday, I've noticed. That don't include you, Ed."

"Well, I just hope if one of them goes in there and bothers the grave you'll give 'em some slack. You handed the preacher a pretty stout warning, and I reminded everybody of it. I've said it before, they're good people, but there's been some remarks."

"I won't take anybody's life, but it's up to them how far down the trail we go."

They talked about the bay pony, how he'd come sauntering up to the stable one day, limping on a hind leg from the bullet he took.

"Your rigging was in good shape, except I could see that the saddle was all scuffed up. Like from the fall you took. And your rifle was still in its scabbard. I've got everything put up for you, so don't worry about it."

"Well, I don't worry about rigging much, but I've wondered about the bullet he took. I reckon it's still in there and I don't know what to do about it."

"Oh, no, the bullet's out. I probed for it and extracted the thing the next day after he walked in."

"Well if you ain't something! Ain't that something. A genuine horse doctor."

"It was a show all right. I had two men on cow ponies use their catch ropes on his forefeet and his hindfeet and we throwed him down and stretched him out. He bellered like a steer, but I popped the lead out anyway, and I believe he'll recover just fine."

188

The news gave Harvey a lift. Caudel left. The ranger considered that the world could be a dark place, but friends sure made a difference. Ed Caudel had been a good one. And he wouldn't forget the Mexican. Antonio. A friend he was not likely to ever see again.

He spent a couple of hours that afternoon working the Neatsfoot Oil into the scuffed gunbelt, wiping it clean and kneading it with his fingers that had become strong and useful again. With the belt done and hanging over a chair he decided his boots could use some of the oil. Boiled from the hooves and bones of cattle, it had been around as long as Harvey could remember. Ed Caudel kept a keg of it in his blacksmith shop, for chaps and saddles and all the rest. Nothing better for leather.

He borrowed a rag from the kitchen and used it to wipe down the Colt revolver and ran it through the barrel to clear out the dust of the cave. He reloaded it and slid it into its holster. It nested there and waited until he would need it again.

Sunday afternoon quiet settled over the town. Not much happening after the church-goers rode off home. Katy had pulled a shift at the cafe. It was the only thing opened up on Sundays, and only for the afternoon. The stores were closed and since Caudel had left, nobody but Morgan Bailey had knocked on his door. She'd brought him a plate of fried potatoes and eggs and said, "This'll be the last of your invalid meals, I think. You look pretty healthy to me."

"Believe I am, and thanks. You took good care of me."

"Well, it was Katy done most of the caretaking. You treat that girl good, mister."

He let some time pass after the remark. "I don't know what you mean."

"Of course you do. Enjoy your meal." The door closed softly and he was alone again.

Katy showed up late in the day, tired and her hair frizzed out a little and stains on her clothes from gravy and spilled coffee and no telling what else. "I need a bath," she said, "before we sit down to supper tonight. You want to come to the table or eat in here again?"

He reflected that life was just that way. There was breakfast and dinner and supper and baths and work and sleep and all over again tomorrow. He was tired of the bed and the rented room and the long days. "I think I'd like to rejoin the living. What do you say?"

Her smile was the thing, the very thing that caused him not to care about the tedium, the suppers and the baths and all the rest. That smile connected him every time he saw it. Connected him to the ground, the sky, the past and the future, and he never wanted to lose it.

CHAPTER 68

Caesar Tims was one of the faces at supper. Dave Mikeska's usual chair was empty. Harvey realized he hadn't seen the artist in days. Tims said, "They tell me you have about licked it."

"You been off somewhere?"

"Little trip." He glanced around the table and got busy eating. That was all he had to say til they'd finished. He wiped his mouth and stood up, pushing back his chair. "That was a fine meal, Morgan." Then to Harvey, "You going back to your room now?"

There was still some daylight left. "I think maybe I'll sit on the porch a while. Fresh air'd be nice."

Katy stayed to help clean up. He took one of the porch chairs and breathed in the fall smells, glad to be alive. A couple of riders went past side by side, headed down to Lou Campbell's. He could hear a far-off whippoorwill calling down at the river bend as night began shading the countryside. He rolled a smoke and remembered the Taps call back at Fort Duncan and the old soldier who'd given him this sack of tobacco. Life sure took its twists and turns. Cee came out. He pulled a chair close.

"I didn't say more because to be honest, I don't like spreading too much information around."

"A trip, you said."

"Yeah. Uvalde and San Antonio. I talked to the sheriff in Uvalde, told him you witnessed the murder and he promised to come down here tomorrow with a deputy."

"They plan to arrest the three men?"

"Well," he said, "I think Braca and Greene for sure, based on your testimony that they beat Deke so badly he died, and

191

then threw his body in the river. Yes, I believe he'll take those two to jail."

"But not Raines?"

Cee shrugged his shoulders. "Sheriff seemed doubtful."

"I heard him give the orders to kill us both."

"I know you did, but you've been a lawman for a long time. You know how the courts are when it comes to evidence. And Raines is a rich man. You know as well as I do that money changes things."

"You're right, I do know that, and I've seen it way more than I've wanted to, but in this case I won't allow it. He'll pay the price for Deke McDonald one way or the other."

"You may get some company from Austin."

That surprised Harvey. He listened to Cee explain that he'd ridden on to San Antonio and sent Western Union telegrams to Ranger Headquarters in Austin, as well as his own home office in Chicago.

"You meant well, but I wish you hadn't done that."

"I felt like you needed somebody to back you up. Hard for one man to fight all of them, and I don't have any right to mix in it. Nor much desire. I'm a plodding artist from the east, not a warrior."

"I thought that was a cover for you."

"No, I mean, it is a cover, but I do paint, and it is my real vocation. In fact, I also sent three of my oils to New York. To the gallery there that shows my work."

Katy came out, still drying her hands on a towel that she dropped in her lap when she took the last chair. Cee said, "I'll go along now. We can talk more tomorrow."

"Will you be around much longer?"

"Maybe not. Our watch on Raines is blown up. I'll have to go back to San Antonio in a while for instructions. Won't know til then." He put his hands on his knees and pushed himself out of the chair with a groan so low Harvey hardly heard it. "Too much time in the saddle."

When he'd gone Harvey scooted the empty chair back a little and Katy brought hers closer. He said, "Does this count as

192

courtin'? I want to do it right but I lack education on the subject."

"I don't know a thing in the world about courting, Harvey." She transferred the damp towel to the empty chair. "And don't much care about it. Seems to me courting is about moonlight and flowers and pipedreams. Nice things, I guess, but you can't live on them. Can't live on sugar and whipped cream. You need meat and potatoes and hot coffee and something sweet from time to time. You need truth and respect. That's what I offer, along with that cobbler you like so much."

"Have I told you that you are a sassy woman?"

"Not that I remember." She was grinning, and he thought that in spite of what she'd said, this was courting, all right.

He added, "And fine looking?" Her teeth shone white in the gloom.

She whispered, "What is it they say? You have a silver tongue?"

"I didn't realize it til now, but you're right. And I have a question for you."

"What is it?"

"Can I borrow a dollar?"

CHAPTER 69

Even though he wore a shirt, his upper body felt naked without the tight bandage wound around and around it. The morning was warm enough to leave off the jacket. His legs felt strong, his footsteps solid as he walked up to the door and knocked. He noted that the numbness was long gone from his hand, but on his wrist a scab outlined the rope burn. The muscles of his chest were sore. He knew he still had to be careful not to overdo things, but a walk over here seemed mild enough.

Lou Campbell's maid stared out at him. She seemed surprised. He held out Katy's silver dollar. "I owe you that."

"You do, yessir, I thought you forgot." The look on her face, her manner, told him more than he could've learned in conversation. She'd thought him dead. He knew it from her startled look. And how could that be? Only if the false news had come here in some form, the form being Fisher Greene, since he believed it true. He hadn't brought it for the ear of this woman, either. No, the news was meant for somebody else, and overheard by this one.

She slipped the money into an apron pocket. "She asleep."

"You reckon Prissy's up yet?"

"She come down for some coffee a while back."

"Can you ask her if she'd come talk to me for a second? I'll be quick."

She was slow to decide just what she ought to do with this man at the door. Her eyes moved up and down him, boots to hat, not focused on him, but seeing possibilities of trouble and herself at fault, letting him in, carrying his request up the stairs. He knew exactly how she was feeling. He remembered the name he'd heard her called by on his first day here.

194

"Do what I'm asking you, Clara." He reached into the shirt pocket and brought out his silver badge, then pinned it on. "This is state business, and I'm telling you to do it. You don't, I'm heading up the stairs and I'll find her myself. Anybody jumps you over it, just say I gave you no choice."

She pulled the door back and let him in. He stood waiting in the parlor where men waited in this house and picked one of the women who were there to be picked. He didn't want to sit on any of the furniture scattered around, didn't want to breathe the coffee-scented air of it.

Katy had offered him the dollar last night, and offered more if he needed it, though he finally convinced her he'd been joking. It pleased him to know that along with all her other qualities she was thrifty, too, and had saved a pile of money from her work at the cafe. What a fine woman. And he'd almost walked right past her. He'd gone to bed remembering Deke McDonald, the little homestead the man had built, the ordered cabin, the garden, the creek that ran behind it all. And the day he'd first seen it, looking for Luther Welty. That was the kind of thing a man ought to aspire to—a place of his own.

The paintings on the wall, the tool Deke had used to crank out the bad tooth while Harvey stood outside, on his way back to Stampede, held up by the arrival of Caesar Tims. It was that picture, all of it, that he carried in his head as he drifted toward sleep and then was asleep and dreaming.

The dreams were scattered and ragged at the edges like scraps of ripped cloth. He woke up many a time in the night, every time one of the scraps had Ella's face on it. Some of the dreams let him sleep on—dreams of people he'd known, a Christmas with cousins come visiting, Ella dancing alone on the porch in the moonlight to music nobody else could hear.

Ella in a room up a long stair. Luther Welty standing there, his tooth hurting him so much it turned his face red. And Luther saying something to him. Something so loud he heard it clearly over the din of a crowd three-deep in this very parlor. Harvey had awakened from it then, quick, like someone had splashed his face with ice water.

One by one the scraps of dreams had unwound and drifted off and left him staring into the dark, and he'd stayed like that til morning came.

CHAPTER 70

She had on a warmer wrap this time, of red flannel, her feet in knitted socks of some dark rusty color. In her hand she carried a cup and from it steam rose. Her eyes were large and a little afraid.

"I thought you was dead."

"Why'd you think that, Prissy?"

"Word was just around, that's all. I don't know, exactly."

"Sit down over here."

"I've got things to do, Harvey. I don't have the time right now."

"Won't take long. I need to ask you a couple of questions."

"Lou won't be happy about it. There'd be a better time and place."

"Sit down."

"I don't think so."

"You talk to me right now or I'll turn customers away from this place til you do."

"What, then? I'll stand right here. Ask your damned questions."

"Fisher Greene a customer of yours?"

"Sometimes."

"He the one told you I was dead?"

"No, somebody told Lou and she's the one spread it around here."

"What about Trey Braca? He been here lately?"

"Both of 'em, yeah." She sipped her coffee, eyes still big over the rim of the cup.

"Where did they go? You know?"

"Wasn't no secret far as I'm aware. Houston, Trey said. He had freight to haul over there."

"Go on back upstairs, Prissy." Lou Campbell was in bad need of her hair combed. Looked like she'd come straight up from the bed and in here mad and half-dressed. Not a bad combination on some women, but no good on this one. "I don't like you coming here this time of day bothering us. I got a business to run. What're you after Prissy for?"

"Appears to me you were running it flat on your back up in your bedroom asleep. Now you're awake and in front of me, I'll ask you what I was about to ask Prissy."

"Go on, then, get it over with."

He slowed himself down. No point letting his voice rise up like a kid. The woman stared at him, waiting. He took a deep breath and let it out. "Back when Ella...when she died...had you hired a new girl? Was somebody new working your crowd that night?"

"Why, no. Why would you ask me that? Got to bring one in now, but we ain't had a new face since...I guess since that Katy girl ran out on me."

Harvey could hear the words from the dream. Luther Welty had said, *nobody prettier, even the new girl.* Words that had slipped right past him on that first visit, with Welty already half-drunk and McDonald getting ready to pull the infected tooth. That's what Harvey'd been trying to remember, what had been nibbling at him all this time. Now Lou Campbell was saying there'd been no new girl, but the young wrangler had seen what he thought was one.

"Fisher tell you I was dead?"

"Nobody said that to me." Her face flushed, the lie obvious.

"He tell you they killed another man?"

"Ain't told me nothing. You heard what I said."

"We both know better, Lou."

He turned to leave. She said, "There's still them clothes upstairs."

Harvey gave it a second's thought and replied, "I'm not finished yet. I'll see to the clothes when I can."

The walk from that house, past Morgan Bailey's place and on to the cafe seemed long and left him ready for an empty chair. He was hungry and the cup of coffee Katy sat in front of him was especially welcome. Her apron was stained and she looked tired already. She dropped into the seat across the small table and leaned forward. "What'll you have, mister?"

"Anything you bring me I'll eat."

She laughed and stood up, pushing back the chair. "There's that silver tongue again. We should get you on the stage, or maybe run you for governor."

"I'd give it all up, Katy, just to be your feller."

Waiting for his food he thought back to what the Campbell woman had told. If it was the truth, and he believed it was, then Luther Welty had made a mistake. He'd been the last to see Ella alive, and going out or coming into that room he'd seen a woman he took to be another one like Ella. All right, another whore like Ella. A new one. Not as pretty as Ella, he'd said.

After long days of no appetite, food tasted good again. His jaw had repaired itself and no longer clicked as he chewed. He vowed to keep himself away from boots and fists from now on. This thing of walking around with bullet holes and sprains and bruises was no way for a man to enjoy life.

CHAPTER 71

Pounding hoofbeats outside got his attention as a frantic team of six horses hauled a wagon up from the river, water flashing off its wheels. Trey Braca pulled them to a hard stop right outside the cafe window. He grabbed a long gun from behind his seat and jumped to the ground. All of it was so quick and unexpected it seemed to Harvey that he was back in the dream from last night. Even as Harvey reached for his own weapon, a built-in reflex, he knew the belt and gun lay draped on a chair in his room across the way. He'd seen no need to walk around armed today.

Braca slammed his way through the door. He carried a double-barreled shotgun and a look of panic. His hat fell off onto the boardwalk. Another horse then, a floundering halt to its gallop and Fisher Greene was out of the saddle and close behind his partner. A rifle fired not far away. Wood splintered off the door facing. Greene raised the pistol in his hand and fired back. The customers inside left their chairs. Some retreated to the kitchen, others to corners of the room, some to the floor. Harvey plucked his hat off the peg behind his chair, put it on and tilted it over his face. He dropped to his knees. Katy came running to him.

Outside, the wagon team pulled their load along the street, away from the cafe. Their long reins trailed in the sand of the street. Greene's horse moved about uncertainly, spooked by the gunfire. Two riders came into sight. When Greene and Braca opened fire on them through the glass window they rode into an alley and came out on foot at a run, splitting up as the shotgun boomed again, more glass shattering. The sound was so loud it deafened Harvey. Around him men and women were yelling or screaming, but their voices were muffled as though by great distance. He held onto Katy, who'd knelt beside him, felt her face burrow into his shoulder, hiding her eyes.

The men outside must be the sheriff and deputy from Uvalde. Harvey had seen the spark of a metal badge on one of them. They'd been on their way here this morning and somewhere came onto the pair they meant to arrest. Surprises all around. Harvey forced his mind back to reality. Greene and Braca were paying no attention to the people inside the cafe. Their attention was on the street, watching for a chance to fire at the lawmen again. Harvey had to do something, change something, move. But how? No weapon and his body not yet over his last tangle with these two. A quick look around, a couple of women in dresses sprawled behind overturned tables. Three men in town clothes, no weapons showing. The young waiter who'd served him once, peering around a corner of the kitchen.

It had to be done and it couldn't wait.

CHAPTER 72

Reloading his shotgun, Trey Braca had to prop it against the wall beside him, his left arm dangling, then he hung the weight of the heavy gun over a crooked elbow. Blood ran down his forearm and soaked the sleeve of his shirt. One of those singing bullets outside had clipped him. Greene emptied his revolver out the window and began to reload. Braca sighted at movement across the street.

"No!" Katy yelled as Harvey left her side and bulled his way toward Braca. Greene glanced back at the sound of her voice and swung his empty pistol at Harvey's head, missing, as the ranger grabbed the shotgun barrel, swung it up at the ceiling and yanked it away. One of the barrels fired close to his right ear and it felt like the ear had been plugged with clay. He knew he'd hurt himself with the move. Pain spasmed across his chest, not from gunfire, but from the bullet wound. Likely torn open again, but there was no time to worry about it.

Katy was right behind him, and Greene's second swipe caught her on the cheek and knocked her down. Before Harvey could come up with the scattergun Greene reached a hand under the neck of his own shirt and came out with an arkansas toothpick. A long, pointed knife, sharpened on two sides that knife fighters carried in a sheath down their backs. He'd holstered his empty revolver. He lifted Katy with his left hand and with his right he put the keen blade to her throat. She was stunned by the blow, her eyes only half-open, confused and unable to resist. Blood fell from a tear in her cheek, dripping onto her apron.

Nothing he could do. That knife would take out her throat, and he didn't doubt for a second that Fisher Greene would do it. Harvey held the shotgun in one hand and let it point to the floor. In front of him now, Braca took it back with his good hand.

Greene said, "Finish him off! Damn that Mexican, anyway!"

"Witnesses, Fisher. Too many eyes. I ain't facing trial for killing no ranger." Braca turned back to the window, but saw no movement.

"Your lucky day, Kitren. This gun of mine was loaded I'd blow you down and to hell with the consequences."

"Let her go. I'll take her place. You can have me."

A cruel twist of the man's lips could have been a smile. "I'll have you, all right. But just not right now. Back away." The long knife quivered at Katy's throat. Her senses were coming back. She understood what was happening.

"I'm sorry, Harvey. I was just trying to..."

"Shut up!" Greene took a good grip in her hair and pulled her tighter against his body. We going on a little walk now. Anybody objects, this whore gets her throat cut. And by god, Kitren! You know I'll do it."

Harvey forced himself to be still, forced himself to ignore the words. He stepped back. Nothing to be done now. Let it play out.

"Me'n Trey and the whore going to walk over to Lou's. Anybody threatens us, I'm plenty quick with this knife."

Braca said, "What about my load?"

"It can set right there til Raines comes after it, Trey."

A few citizens had come out of their stores and houses to see about the ruckus. Curious eyes watched the pair of outlaws and the captive woman stop in the middle of the street. The men argued, Braca shaking his head and nodding toward the wagon and work team. Greene kept his grip on Katy, the hateful knife at her throat. The sheriff and deputy emerged from behind watering troughs, one in front of the general store and another one farther down the street. Both held revolvers, pointed down. Nobody wanted Katy harmed if it could be helped.

CHAPTER 73

Greene yelled out, and Harvey could just make out the words. "Put 'em down, men. I'll slice her. I'll slice her." Elbow raised and wrist cocked, ready to carry it out and die himself in the process. They each bent down and laid their weapons in the dust.

Harvey gritted his teeth, his mouth full of the rotten taste of anger and fear for Katy, and frustration with himself for letting this happen. The knife. That long and shiny knife. A memory sliced through his own thoughts, a picture of long ago, him in bed just waking up, and in the distance, through the boards and windows of his house, the sound of hogs squealing, bleeding out with cut throats, men shouting, the smell of winter in the air. Slaughter time. It happened every year back then. He shook the memory out of his head.

Then, it looked like Greene changed his mind and forced Katy ahead, moving along behind Braca to the freight wagon. Braca put the shotgun on the wagon seat and climbed aboard using his good hand to pull himself up. He sat down, then realized he'd left the reins trailing in the street. Harvey watched him curse himself, climb back down and do it all over again holding the leather strips in his teeth.

Fisher Greene had said he was headed to Lou Campbell's house, but now they'd taken a different route. Harvey walked outside for a better look. Pushing Katy along beside the wagon, Greene noticed him come out and made another gesture of threat with the knife. Harvey spread his arms and opened his hands to make sure the man understood he carried no weapon.

As the wagon rolled on down the street the two from Uvalde came over to Harvey. He recognized the sheriff from his earlier visits to that office. A youngish fellow named Carel. He couldn't remember the man's first name. Nor did that matter. All that mattered right now was getting Katy away from Greene's knife. The deputy looked a little older than Carel. A short, dark-skinned man with a beard that hid half his face. Carel said, "This here's my deputy. Ruben." The short man offered his hand. Harvey accepted it with a nod. It felt thick and powerful in his grip.

Sheriff Carel went on, "You ain't armed either, I see. Ain't this pitiful, three of us standing here without weapons. We have purely blundered our way through the day so far."

Harvey saw Fisher Greene's abandoned horse standing like a statue a few feet away. A rifle sheath was strapped to the saddle and it held a lever-action of some sort. He said, "I hope that's loaded." The horse backed away from him as he walked toward it. "Whoa now. Whoa." The animal was a pretty one, carrying some palomino blood, looked like. A gelding, brown coat and lighter mane and tail. He got a hand on the bridle and pulled the rifle out it its sheath. The chamber was empty, but the magazine was full. So he was armed now. Seemed strange Greene had left the horse, and stranger still the gun, but he'd been rattled, not thinking straight. Harvey slid the rifle back into its sheath and put a hand on the saddle horn.

He ignored the bad pains in his chest, knowing he'd hurt himself back in the cafe. It could not matter now. Katy mattered, and that was all of it. He stepped into a stirrup shushing the horse's shyness, talking to him, and rose into the saddle. "I'm going after them," he told Carel.

"Hang on. Ruben, get the weapons, will you? I'll round up our horses."

CHAPTER 74

The wagon was out of sight, just past the place where the street bent. Katy, too, was out of sight. He let the nervous gelding pace a few steps, then reined him in a circle, waiting for the others. He had plenty of questions for Carel, but they could wait.

Finally the three rode abreast along the sandy avenue and saw Trey Braca guide his team into the stable yard. Greene kept his hostage close, his knife arm poised. Harvey had no doubt the vengeful man would take out his hatred on her, innocent and defenseless as she was. He saw Greene glance back at the trio on horseback just as Ed Caudel came out the door.

The blacksmith paused, wiping his hands with a cloth, taking in the scene, his posture one of surprise. They were too far to hear voices, but Fisher was handing out orders, no doubt about that. Ed nodded and walked toward the corral. Probably going after another mount for the big man. But no, he opened the gate and shooed the loose horses inside away from the gap. Braca drove his wagon through the gate and stopped it beside a back building. Braca stepped down holding his shotgun, pointing it in Ed's direction. Caudel raised his arms over his head. Braca said something and the blacksmith nodded toward a door. Braca walked to the door and opened it, keeping his gun trained on Ed Caudel.

Greene used a knee against Katy's hip to shove her along in front of him toward the door. Harvey saw movement inside that dark doorway. He knew it led into Caudel's tack room, where saddles, bridles and the like were kept. But something white filled it now. The dog. Deke's white dog walked out the door and stood looking around at the commotion. His hindquarters seemed to have mended. His walk was normal. Braca came around with his gun and fired at the animal. The explosion sounded loud as all creation, but the lead shot flew into empty space.

The dog had launched himself at Fisher Greene.

Harvey whipped the rifle out of its sheath and dug his heels into his horse's flanks. He sensed the other two men close behind, but all his attention just then was on Katy. Too much was happening. He felt like he was riding through a lake of quicksand, trying to get to her, trying to get close enough to save her. Ed Caudel dove for the gun just fired by Braca, yanked it away from the freighter and used it to knock him to the ground.

The white dog had Greene by the knife arm, tearing at him with teeth that looked longer and sharper than the toothpick. Katy dropped to the ground and quickly got herself up on hands and knees and scuttled away. Harvey jerked the horse to a halt and jumped to the ground jacking a shell into the rifle chamber.

He had Greene in his sights, but the big dog was so close, moving in such a furious burst of energy and hate he held off, fearful of hitting it. Then he caught movement in the corner of his eye and Ed Caudel tore into the picture with the shotgun he'd just taken away from Braca. Quick steps, a hard swing, and the heavy barrels slammed into the back of Greene's head. And that was it. Greene dropped like an empty sack. The only sound then was the growling and barking of the Pyrenees that had his own idea of how this ought to end.

CHAPTER 75

She held onto him for a long time. He stroked her hair while she cried into his shoulder. Blood was smeared on her neck and stained the front of the blouse she wore. He noted the sharp edge of the knife where it lay and felt tempted to give Greene a taste of what he'd just done to this young woman. Carel and his deputy shifted the gun crates enough to get Fisher Greene and Trey Braca into the freight wagon. Braca was still unconscious from the lick on his head. Greene was drifting in and out, his eyes and his understanding not focused.

A crowd had followed the action along the street, and a few of the people came forward now. Morgan Bailey was one of them. She said, "I prayed all the way down here. Ed's my new hero." She pulled Katy loose from Harvey and hugged her close. "Let's me and you go back home and put something on that cut." Morgan was a head shorter than the girl, who looked back at Harvey once then let herself be taken away.

He let the tangle of feelings and thoughts roll around in his head and his belly while he went to where Ed Caudel stood with the tall dog, looking a little confused and not at all like a hero. Harvey put a hand on the blacksmith's shoulder and heard a low growl. He removed his hand.

Caudel said, "That pony of yours is doing good."

"Wanted to thank you, and the dog, too, I guess, for saving Katy just now."

"Just now. Yeah. I feel like I worked hard all day. That was all so..." He trailed off.

The wagon team stood with their heads down, no energy left in their movements. They'd come into town at a hard run and had not yet recovered from it. The loose horses, including Harvey's, had gathered in a corner of the pen and watched the goings on in an uninterested manner, as if men and women and their constant turmoil were unworthy of attention.

The deputy, Ruben, had rolled both prisoners onto their bellies and handcuffed their arms behind them. The cuffs he used were of a new sort that adjusted to the wearer's wrist size and held him securely. Harvey noticed it and said to the sheriff, "How'd you come by the cuffs? I've never liked using them, they're always too little or too big for a prisoner."

Carel said, "Yeah, it's a new one. I bought 'em a year ago, had 'em shipped in." He pointed to Braca. "This character right here brought 'em."

That was a satisfying thing. And it was even more satisfying that those two were in the exact situation He'd been in not long ago, along with Deke McDonald. Arms locked behind their backs, jostling overland with a load of guns.

The sheriff was red in the face, from a combination of effort and danger and maybe a little shame. "Me and Ruben messed up, and I'm sorry about it all. We chanced on these two a few miles back. They'd spent the night, it looked like. Must've come up the Camino Real and stopped to rest. I didn't recognize soon enough who they were, so that's on me. Next thing I know, they're shooting at us and on the way here."

"So you plan to haul 'em to jail now? The wood crates in the wagon are guns, belong to Roy Raines, as I expect you'll find out soon."

"Yeah, judge wouldn't give me a warrant without talking to you first. I'd like you to come up pretty soon and make a statement. I can hold onto 'em a few days anyway, just on their behavior today. As far as the guns, if they bought 'em fair and square then I got no say-so about it. Besides, Raines has got his fingers in all the pudding out here. It's a rare event things go against him."

"How about you? His fingers on you?"

"It's a fair question, but no. I'm one of the rare events."

"Leave the guns here with Ed. I'll ride up in a day or two and talk to the judge. And it may be you can get enough out of these two to arrest Raines for murder. They might be in the

209

mood to bargain. I can add to that. Plus, I think he killed off one of his ranch hands. No proof yet, but I'm looking."

Caudel helped them offload the crates and stack them inside the tack room. Harvey watched the work, his chest hurting, hoping the recent damage was not too bad. They finished, and made ready to leave.

Carel said, "What about that palomino? Want me to trail him back with us?"

Harvey said, "Leave him here, why don't you. My ride is still under the weather and I could use him right now." He felt rooted where he stood. The procession moved gradually out of sight, Ruben driving the work team, the animals lifting their heavy hooves in a slow dance, all of them, men and beasts, wrung out and weary with the day.

The white dog watched Caudel shut the gate and come back inside the pen. The blacksmith looked older, his walk slower than Harvey had noticed before. He said, "Believe I'll go sit down awhile, Harvey. You ought to do the same." They looked at one another in silence and shook hands.

"You named that dog yet?"

"No hurry. It'll come."

CHAPTER 76

"You might should see Doc Pruett again," Morgan Bailey said when they'd all sat down for supper that night. All but Dave Mikeska. His chair was empty again.

Harvey said, "Maybe not. Katy says it looks okay to her, and it don't hurt much now."

The old woman said, "What is it about men and doctors? I never did understand it. My husband, God rest his soul, seemed like he'd rather expire than see one."

Harvey swallowed a bite of stewed peas and said, "Sounds about right to me."

Katy went through her meal in an absent-minded way, like her attention was somewhere else. She'd been like that all afternoon, and he thought it was a normal thing for her to be distracted from life around her, focused on what had happened to her, how close she'd come to dying with that knife at her throat. Her throat was bandaged. Their landlady had taken care of that early in the day, and had also helped her bathe and change into clean clothes. She looked just fine, but her manner indicated the need for time to get past the fear she'd endured today.

She went with him to the porch and sat beside him while he rolled a smoke. The air was cold. She shivered. "I'm tired, Harvey. Think I'll go on to bed."

"Sun's barely down." He liked the feel of her close by, hated to let her get away even that far, knowing it was selfish, but not exactly minding that it was. He put his hand on her arm and squeezed it softly, feeling the goose bumps on her skin. "You go on if that's what you want. Just holler if you need me. I won't be far."

211

He rolled and smoked another cigarette after she left, liking the feel of cold on his face, content in some ways, but still worried that he had no leads on Ella's killer except for that knife. Time had slipped past him and maybe now he'd have to leave here with that savagery unresolved. A horse and rider went past the house. He couldn't see them. The night had turned dark with just a sliver of moon. Nothing but the tread of hooves and the jingle of spurs marked the passage. Then a wavering light appeared, moving his direction, coming closer. It was a lantern, somebody carrying it, hurrying, then turning in. A man he recognized held it high enough to light his own face and see Harvey sitting to one side of the porch. He'd never heard the man's name, but had seen him swamping the floor of the Frio saloon.

"They sent me looking for Dave Mikeska," he said, "Time for him to be at work and nobody's seen him."

Harvey said, "Same here, I guess. He was not at supper."

"They'll want to know if I looked in his room. Can I?"

"I don't see why not." Harvey left the cool night air and the sliver of moon and led the fellow down the hallway to the door of Mikeska's room. He knocked and got no answer, opened the door and looked inside. The swamper stepped up beside him and raised the lantern. Harvey smelled kerosene and the burning wick and noted the moving shadows it threw across the empty room. Nobody home.

CHAPTER 77

The thoughts were at him when he opened his eyes, the sun not up, night still sitting on the town like a brooding hen. They came after him like mosquitoes. Where was the Welty boy? Who killed Ella? Would the church people leave her grave alone? What about Katy? Would she be all right? Would she have him if he asked her to marry him? Would her past interfere with that? "No," he said out loud. And it would not. He hadn't even thought about it since the second she'd walked in the door down at Fort Duncan. Not once. No, it was settled for him. Maybe not for her, but that was something to yet be learned.

He dressed and walked down to Caudel's stable looking for a cup of coffee. Most of the fresh pain he'd felt in his chest after that business yesterday had left him. So maybe he hadn't hurt himself too much after all.

The big white dog was standing beside the blacksmith when Harvey came through the door. Caudel put a hand on the wide head and shushed the growl.

"You're an ungrateful animal," Harvey said. "I deserve better." He offered the back of his hand for a sniff and saw the heavy tail wag once. "How are you, Ed?"

"Better, I'd say. Took a while, but I'm about back all the way."

"Well, you saved the day, you and whatchacallit here. Hadn't been for you, no telling what those fools would've done." He poured himself a cup from the burnt pot. "Pony okay?"

"He's out there with the rest. I haven't looked close up yet, but I think so."

Harvey carried his coffee to a side door and went into the horse pen. He found his horse and ran his hand over the wound, barely visible in the new dawn. His hand carried away the stink of worm medicine. "Glad we didn't have to part company," he said. "Get plenty of rest. We got to head back to Austin before long." The little bay turned his head and looked directly at Harvey as if he understood what he'd just been told. Fisher Greene's palomino stood beside the back fence, a reminder that they'd be expecting him in Uvalde soon. Well, it wouldn't be today. He planned to stick close to Katy in case she needed him. Hoped she would.

Inside, he rinsed the cup with a dipper of water and told Caudel, "Think I'll take a look over at the cemetery." On the way out he remembered the missing Dave Mikeska. he said, "Fellow over at the boarding house has disappeared. Worked at the saloon? Any chance he rented a horse from you?"

"Dave, you mean? No, he kept one here, though. A nice black gelding. Rode it from California he told me. The horse is gone, so he might have come in yesterday and got him. Manuel would know. I can ask him."

He left thinking that the white-bearded man and the white dog made a nice looking pair. And it seemed like the dog was something Ed needed, filled an empty spot. Harvey had never even asked or wondered if Caudel had a wife. Or kids. He'd have to remember to make a point of inquiring. And where in the world had Mikeska gone off to?

CHAPTER 78

Empty and quiet. No surprise at this time of day. And easy to see that there'd been some mischief. They'd kept it from him, no doubt fearing he'd go on a rampage. And he might have. But that sort of thing seemed to be in the past along with the rest of the feelings he'd put there. There'd been some black paint, because you could see a little of it still deep in a few of the letters where they couldn't wipe it out. The smell of turpentine was faint but still in the quiet air, so the cleanup had not been too long done. Yesterday, he supposed.

In the main, his interest focused on the vase of flowers that sat beside Ella's gravestone. The stems of three sunflowers crowded into the narrow neck of a clear glass receptacle. Someone had filled the vase with water to keep the flowers alive longer, the blooms themselves each as large as a man's hand. Big, yellow-orange things that seemed too cheerful for the work they were assigned. The Ella he remembered best, the young one, the growing one, would have liked them. One of the women at Lou's, he guessed. Prissy, maybe.

Walking back, thinking he'd look in on Katy, hoping she was over the scare of yesterday, he took out his sack of tobacco and realized it was nearly empty. He shifted his route in the sandy street and headed for the general store. The clerk was behind his counter. What was his name? Forsythe? Harvey felt a little pity for the man, married as he was to a cold lizard of a woman.

"I've run out," he said, tossing the nearly empty sack on the counter. "No telling what I'd a done if you wasn't open for business."

When Forsythe turned away to get out a sack of Bull Durham Harvey saw, on a shelf beside the cash drawer, a pot of flowers, the same sunflowers he'd just found at the grave. The sight left him stunned. He fumbled in his pocket for money. "Pretty flowers there," he said.

Forsythe made change and said, "Yes, thanks. Not many plants bloom this late in the year. We always keep a patch of these and shield them from the cold long as possible. Pearl likes flowers around us."

He felt awash in uncertain water. There were, in the blink of an eye, answers he'd come to this town for, right in front of him, and yet he hesitated to start the chase.

"Your wife put the bouquet on Ella's grave? I was just now over there." Forsythe had turned pale as ashes.

Harvey could see the agony in the man's eyes. "No...I did...last night."

"Well, I guess you knew my sister, then."

"I...did, yes."

Harvey was quick making the leap in logic, and saw no point in dancing around it. He'd recovered from the shock of seeing the flowers. His head was clear. "You the one she stayed here for?"

Forsythe backed away and Harvey recognized the look of fear. "I ain't going to come after you. Just answer me."

"I loved her."

"Another question, and you had damned well better tell me the truth. Did you kill her?" He was thinking of the knife he'd found in that shed between this store and Lou's. Somebody coming here could've put it there and kept right on to that side door on the alley and been out of sight quick.

Forsythe's face seemed to melt. His mouth twisted and tears glittered in his eyes. "No no no no no no." His head swung side to side. "Never."

Harvey believed him. And not only that...the pieces of it slid into place as he remembered Luther Welty's words. *The new girl.*

"Your wife?"

The man doubled over, like he'd been kicked in the stomach. He gagged but nothing came up. He swallowed and said, "Maybe. I don't know for sure."

"She learned about you and Ella and she went over one night when it was loud and busy and she killed her. She hid the knife she used in Morgan Bailey's shed, where I found the thing."

Forsythe took a deep breath and seemed to calm down a little. "She knew. I told her, when I found out she was going out to that...to Roy Raines. I told her when she wouldn't stop it."

So there it was. You never knew when you'd stumble across the answers, or where they'd come from. "If you loved her and she loved you, then why didn't you take her out of that place?" Harvey was whispering now, but his heart pounded in his ears. "How can you tell me you loved a woman that was whoring for a living and you left her on her own? It does not make any sense to me."

"I put it off, is all. I put it off. A day at a time." Harvey considered the answer and while it was self-serving, it was also true of much of the hurt and evil loose in the world. People unwilling or afraid to deal with today's need today.

"Where's your wife?"

He stared down at the floor. "I'm not sure. She saddled her horse after church Sunday and rode off. To Raines, I guess. I have not seen her since." This fellow had more than one heavy load to carry. Hard times were coming.

"She keep her horse at the stable?" Maybe Ed Caudel had some idea where she went.

"No. At our place. We've got a little pasture, out west of town."

"And you're sure she's not at home."

"I ain't sure of nothing."

CHAPTER 79

She wasn't there. Harvey had directions from Forsythe. The palomino seemed happy for a chance to stretch his legs. He rode back toward Stampede, thinking of Katy and maybe some breakfast with her at the cafe. She could be over there now, working. He hoped not. She needed another day of rest.

He had no doubts that Pearl Forsythe was the killer he'd come to find. And who'd twice tried to do the same to him. It fit with everything he'd learned. The answer as to why the thing between Ella and the store clerk had worked its way into being wasn't going to come easily. Maybe never. Even the man who'd admitted it didn't seem to know the hows and whys of it. Separation. Death. There ought to be more. There ought to be the sound of thunder and clouds full of reasons that rained down. His feelings were a mixture of the always-present grief over Ella's death, the satisfaction of having assembled the scraps of it into a whole piece, the way he always felt at the end of a hunt, and the raw edge of unfinished work. A killer was still loose.

He was near town when he reined the horse south and took the trail that would lead him to the Double R.

Sheriff Carel might be on his way, or might come tomorrow, might have some paper that would mean arrest for Roy Raines, but it was unlikely. The other two wouldn't give him up. They'd hold on and stay quiet, figuring Raines would use his money and connections to get them out of the mess they'd made. There was no way Raines could know Harvey was alive, instead of in a shallow grave somewhere in Mexico. Alive to testify of Raines' orders. No way, except for the

218

Forsythe woman. She was out here no doubt, but had she even known about Harvey when she left town? He didn't think so.

The sun felt thin on his back, rising up toward noontime with a cool wind blowing. When he reached the headquarters he freed the rifle and balanced it across the pommel of the saddle. He gentled the horse down to a walk and went forward to the house.

Wood smoke flavored the wind that met him. There'd be a cook fire in that building off to the left, making a meal for cowhands due in here soon. No commotion that he could see. Nobody moving around. Closer, he recognized the figure of a man in a rocking chair on the porch. Raines? No, it was the cook, or the one he thought of as the cook. The man kept his seat and watched Harvey ride up and dismount. He carried the rifle over his left elbow with his right hand near the trigger guard. Pearl Forsythe was here somewhere and he was ready to shoot first if he saw her, woman or not.

"That's Fisher's horse you're on. Where's he at?"

The voice seemed loud in the strange quiet that surrounded this house. "Where's Raines? Where's the Forsythe woman?"

"I asked you where's Fisher."

"Stand up." Harvey let the rifle barrel move in the cook's direction. "Put your hands behind your head." The man ignored him. He stayed in the rocking chair and his hands remained in his lap. His behavior didn't seem like resistance or a threat. More like he was sad, or confused, or maybe both.

"Ain't worth shooting you over, I guess. But tell me right now, where's Raines?"

"Everything you want is right through that door."

"All right." He climbed the steps and caught the cook by his collar with one hand, holding onto the rifle with the other. He forced him out of the chair and toward the door. "You go on through. Open it slow. I'm right behind you."

It was quick. Three or four steps and Harvey was standing on some kind of big rug. Sunshine through the windows lit the room, but it felt cold inside, colder than the porch. And the cook had told the truth. Everything he wanted was right there.

219

CHAPTER 80

Pearl Forsythe sat in one of the chairs. She wore a blue dress and had no weapon that he could see. Her face held the same look, a mixture of sadness and confusion.

On the floor at her feet lay what had been Roy Raines. Part of his skull was missing and blood had soaked into the rug around him. Harvey smelled the coppery scent of it. And somethng else was evident. The blood was dried.

"When did this happen?" He said. The woman didn't even look up, as if she hadn't heard. Maybe she hadn't. Without turning to face him, the cook said, "She's been like that for two days now. Ain't said word one to nobody."

"Well, I'm sort of confused. Who shot him? And when?"

"*When* was yesterday about this time, maybe a little earlier. I was in the cook shack and I heard the shot but I didn't come checking right away. You know how these crazy ranch hands behave. I didn't think much about it. Then I seen that man ride off so I come to see, and here he was."

"What man?"

"Stranger to me. I didn't know him. He come in early and talked to the boss in the house is all I know."

"What'd he look like?"

"Well, tall and skinny, I guess. Rode a nice looking black horse."

That answered one of the questions that had been bothering Harvey. But why would Dave Mikeska ride out here and shoot Raines?

"You sure it wasn't this woman here?"

"Well, Ranger, she was somewhere around. It's hard to be sure, and she ain't said nothing, but I'd bet money it was the skinny feller."

"He was the bartender from town." Pearl Forsythe had decided to talk. She stood up. Harvey noticed her feet were bare. He'd forgotten to hate her, but it came back quick enough.

Harvey told her, "Sit back down."

"I was going to show you."

"What?"

"The strongbox in that corner over there." She pointed to a square metal box with a lock hanging loose on the hinged lid.

Harvey looked into the empty box, keeping her in the corner of his vision, wishing he had handcuffs with him. "What about it?"

"Dave got the drop on Roy and made him bring that thing out of the back and open it up. Said it belonged to him. There was cash—a lot of cash, and papers that he took. He talked about a gold mine in California that Roy stole from him. Claimed Roy killed his partner. Then, he just...he just shot Roy. In cold blood."

Harvey decided to give more thought to the story at a later time. Nobody knew the root source of Raines' wealth. Maybe it was stolen California gold. Right now, he had this murdering woman to deal with. He told the cook, "I want you to go get her horse and saddle it. Or find somebody else can do it."

"You ain't gonna hurt her, are you?"

"I'm arresting her, and I'll add you to it if you get in my way. Now do what I said."

To Pearl, "Get yourself into some riding clothes." He followed her down a short hall into another room. A Winchester rifle was propped in a corner. He levered the shells out and laid it empty across her bed. "Get your clothes on."

"Not with you watching, I won't."

"You're nothing to me but a murderous witch, not a woman at all, and I got no interest. I'll look right past you, and if you give me a single excuse I'll shoot you dead. Do it."

CHAPTER 81

He left the body of Raines as it lay. It ought to hold up another day in this cold weather before it started to rot. Or decompose, as they said in polite circles. Whatever they called it, rich man or poor man, a body rotted. Sheriff Carel could get out here before then.

They rode to Stampede in silence. The woman had nothing to say and he had no interest in talking to her. She'd already told him back at the house enough for him to put it together. Thinking of Dave Mikeska almost made him smile. He wished that strange man a safe journey. Far as Harvey was concerned justice had been served. He hoped that strongbox had held a lot of cash.

Riding through town, the smell of cooking hung in the air, reminding him he'd had nothing to eat all day, but he had no appetite, and no desire to stop. As they went past the general store he saw her look at it. What would be the thoughts going through the head of a woman like that? Singing like an angel in church and doing murder other times.

Opposite the cemetery he halted the horses and said, "That's her grave right over yonder. There's flowers on it your husband put there. She was wrong in some ways, but she never hurt nobody. Not on purpose, anyway. For what you did to her, I plan to do all I can to see you hanged."

They took her off his hands in Uvalde. Sheriff Carel said, "We'll do our best, but I'd like more evidence against her."

"Greene and Braca know what she's done. Squeeze 'em, now that Raines is gone. They won't be so coy when they find out. It'd help to get a statement from Luther Welty, about seeing her there that night, but I fear the boy is dead. You want to keep her horse here?"

"Yeah. I'll hold it as evidence."

"Nice horse."

"Good evidence. What about Greene's palomino?"

"Same thing. I got plans to take him up to Austin if things work out. You can have him after that."

Carel said, "I don't believe I know what you're talking about."

Harvey said, "That's okay." He got directions to the county judge's office. When they finished with him he stopped off at the clerk's office and then rode back to Stampede alone.

When he sat down to supper at last he felt almost too tired to eat. Katy seemed better, her throat covered by a clean white bandage. He told the news of the day between bites of mashed potatoes and fried chicken and mustard greens and later pound cake with strong coffee. There was surprise around the table. And questions, some of which he answered and to some of which there was no answer possible. He felt some vitality coming back, along with a hum of excitement. Ed Caudel had joined them for the meal, sitting in the chair once occupied by Dave Mikeska. Ed had changed out of his work clothes and looked ready for a church service. Clean shirt and black string tie.

They were finished up. Katy left her chair to begin carrying dishes away from the table. Morgan said to her, "Sit back down."

"But I need to..."

"The ranger fellow has somethng to say to you. Sit."

True, Harvey had not felt much fear in his life, though he'd spent many years of it in constant danger. He felt it now. Katy looked at him, waiting. All of them were quiet, Rosa, next to him, Cee Tims and Ed across the table.

He met her eyes. "Katy, I want...will you...will you marry me?"

"What?" She covered her eyes. It was a surprise, all right. He waited. She lowered her hand. Her lips quivered.

"You know I will."

"Right this minute?"

"There's things to do if..."

"I've done 'em. Done 'em all. He pulled the marriage license from his pocket, the one he'd brought back from Uvalde today.

"What about a preacher? Or a judge or somebody?"

"This great state of ours says any church officer can do it. Friend Ed here is a deacon at that little outpost across the way."

"You want Ed to marry us?"

"He took a bath and put on a necktie. He's ready. How about you?"

They did it, standing beside the table, and then everybody talked loud and laughed and ate more cake and drank coffee and Harvey felt like for the first time in a long time his world had turned right side up.

CHAPTER 82

Harvey watched the months pass by like the ripples in the Colorado River that flowed not far from the house they'd rented. Summer was half done, winter still a few months away. Katy had put his breakfast on the table and he was ready to report in to his captain within the hour. He read the letter again. It came the day before by stage. The Uvalde County Sheriff wrote in an even, clear hand the news that Luther Welty was alive after all. Instead of murdering him, Roy Raines had given him some money and advised him to go elsewhere. Which he'd done for a while, then heard about Raines' fate and come back to work for Doc Pruett, who'd paid the back taxes on the place and taken it over. All that bunch—Greene, Braca, the woman—were headed for trial at last. There was ample evidence to convict them all, assuming the trial jury was sane, which was not always a sure thing.

"You don't have to go back for the trial, do you?"

Katy sipped her coffee and pretended the answer was not important. She'd gained a little weight in the last year and it looked good on her. She didn't have to work so hard now with just the two of them and the house to look after. She had few good memories of the town of Stampede.

"Not according to this letter." He'd only had to leave Austin a couple of times since he'd come back, once to look into cattle rustling over on the eastern side of the state, the other a riot down in Laredo. Over what, he'd never been certain. He had not liked being away from her. He'd asked for somethng permanent that would keep him in Austin. Or, another location would be all right just so he could see his bride every night when work was done.

When he showed up at headquarters Captain Burton asked to see him.

"Have you seen the paper?" Burton asked.

"This week? No, sir."

Burton spread the paper, The Democratic Statesman, on his desk. The headline was big and dark. *Juarez Dead.* It went on to tell that the long-time leader of Mexico had died and a power struggle was going on. There was strong support for General Diaz, the hero of the battle of Puebla, but nothing was assured.

"I have a deal for you. You asked for permanent assignment, now that you're a married man. There's an opening for someone qualified to serve as security for Governor Davis. You can have the job, if you want it."

Everything always came with strings attached. Davis was no friend of the Rangers. Harvey didn't like his politics. Nor did he care for him personally. There was talk, though, that Davis wouldn't last much longer.

"But first, there's another chore I want you to do." More strings.

"There's a strong feeling in Texas that our welfare would be best served if General Diaz is the next Mexican president. To that end, some people have outfitted a couple of wagon loads of guns. They're set to leave in a week for El Paso. Nothing illegal about it. "Nothing *very* illegal, anyhow. The Mexicans will meet the wagons on this side of the border." Burton shook his head. "It's got the governor's blessing. I want three of you along as protection, you as lead man. After this, the Austin job's yours if you want it. Your contact down there is some wild-eyed revolutionary by the name of Flores—Antonio Flores."

Sundays were always quiet around town. There were church services and family gatherings, fishing in the Colorado, swimming in the cold water of Barton Springs in the summertime. He and Katy hadn't yet overcome their aversion to sermons. They took long walks sometimes, just the two of them, and sometimes they took along a picnic basket. Other times they rode horses or rented a buggy.

Today they rode west out into the hills, Harvey on his bay pony, Katy on the palomino they were never going to give back. He had no particular destination in mind when they left, but talking about the job offer and the planned expedition took his attention and required a good deal of time. She didn't like it any better than the last time he'd left her alone, but liked the prospect of permanence later. Harvey wanted that security job. And he wanted to see Antonio again.

Before he realized how far they'd come, they crossed the narrow creek where Harvey had long years back tossed away a silver ingot shaped like an iguana. The Pedernales River was just over the next hill. He told her about his trip out to Junction City, investigating the death of a crooked lawman,

She insisted they get down and look for the silver. They waded barefoot in the cold water for an hour, crossing back and forth, edge to edge. They didn't find it. Harvey was glad about that. The day had been a good one. He felt at peace. They rode home.

www.ingramcontent.com/pod-product-compliance
Lightning Source LLC
Chambersburg PA
CBHW070624130626
46556CB00001B/469